I0722396

CITY

OF

LIGHT AND SUN

A COMPANION NOVELLA TO

THE ORDER OF THE CRYSTAL DAGGERS

◊　　◊　　◊　　◊

C. S. Johnson

1ˢᵗ Edition.
eBook ISBN: 978-1-948464-69-7
Paperback ISBN: 978-1-948464-70-3
Hardback ISBN: 978-1-948464-71-0

AUTHOR'S QUICK NOTE:

This book is set after the story and before the epilogue in *Heart of Hope and Fear*, Book 3 of The Order of the Crystal Daggers, but it can be read as a standalone adventure for Ben and Marguerite.

This book is first dedicated to Sam. It might be tradition at this point, but the point is still there, and I still know why it's there, too.

Second, this book is for my dear friend Kevin, and his soon-to-be-wife, Laura! *Cảm ơn,* for the help with the translation work, *ban.*

Finally, this book is also dedicated to all the people who, like me, where unwilling to let the series go without one last huzzah: Terri, Laura, Gay, Anne, Pat-Charis, William, Jennifer, and Cathy, Rebecca, Priscila, Darla, Donna, Rebecca B., Priscila, Tina, and Carla, and Anne.

C. S. JOHNSON

1

◊

Paris, 1874

"Ben."

It was always an exceptional case when I failed to hear Marguerite calling for me. In the short years since we'd met, my wife's voice had become a necessary sound to my world; it was music to my soul, a bulwark against all the darkness and pain in the world as much as it was a foretaste of heavenly pleasure.

I did not ignore it lightly.

But at just that moment, I found myself in the middle of a grand Parisian bookshop, and my attention was understandably divided. I glanced upward, scanning the high, wooden shelves around me, and gazing at the upper levels of bookcases, all housed underneath a high vaulted ceiling. After days traveling at sea, it was not only the books that captivated and steadied me.

Standing there, I was transfixed by a ghostly, otherworldly sense, one full of certainty and strength.

I closed my eyes and let the wonder wash over me.

Somehow, unexplainably, I knew my mother had once been in this shop.

Máma.

My mother had been lost at sea when I was just a boy. Since then, I clung to what I could remember of her.

I could picture her in my mind, with her hair long and dark, smooth and straight. Against fashion and convention, she'd often worn it down, letting it frame her face and fall behind her. I could see her eyes, blue as the sky, as they clouded over with secrets.

I never quite knew what she was thinking, but never did I question her love for me—or her love for my sister, Ella, or her love for my father. It was a constant light, hovering over us, all throughout our time together. After she died, that essence remained, its presence as real and certain as her absence.

She loved us with that same, supernatural assurance I felt standing in the small, cluttered bookshop.

I opened my eyes, both elevated and deflated; it was though I'd been welcomed home, only to find myself more homesick than ever.

I bit back a sigh. I'd lost more than my mother when she died.

"Ben."

Marguerite tugged on my sleeve, and I turned to face her.

Despite my mood, I gave her a small smile. There was a poetic symmetry in her delicacy, one that contrasted sharply with her assertive nose, her green-glittered eyes, and her loose, persistent blonde curls. She was in many ways the perfect counterpart for me; she had optimism to battle my cynicism, and sweetness to balance out my surliness.

"What is it?" I asked.

"Is this the one you were looking for?" She held out a copy of *Morte d'Arthur,* and the familiarity of the bright scarlet cover immediately caught my attention.

At once, an old memory came to mind.

I could see the same book in *Máma's* hand as she pleaded with *Otec* to read it aloud to the rest of us. Cheerfully, as much as reluctantly, he read at her insistence, ruffling his

THE ORDER OF THE CRYSTAL DAGGERS

mustache as he flipped through the pages. I sat in *Máma*'s lap as Ella squirmed in front of us on the library floor.

After *Máma* died, *Otec*'s approval of me seemed to die along with her. He no longer read much, except when Ella asked. He never willingly denied my mother anything, and Ella looked so much like her, I imagined the habit was too hard for him to break.

And after I broke my leg, leaving me with a permanent limp, what had been broken between me and my father further shattered into dust.

Still, as Marguerite pressed the book into my hands, I touched the leather cover reverently. Taking a deep breath, I opened it up, and there, inside the back cover, was my father's firm penmanship.

"To Benedict, who I am proud——"

I exhaled sharply.

A new layer of stitching had been added to the cover, likely in the last year or two. The lining's small little strips of thread obscured the rest of the inscription, although I could still recite the words by heart:

"to call my son. May the blessings of strength, wisdom, and courage follow you throughout life. Your Father, Adolf Svoboda."

The dedication was brief before it was cut off, and then, the pain of the past was covered and tended to by others' hands; *Otec* and his affection for me had suffered a similar fate. In the end, it was disappointing, but also fitting.

Marguerite cleared her throat behind me. "Is it the right one?"

"This is it." I nodded, both grateful and conflicted by its rediscovery. "This is the one I promised my sister I would find."

THE ORDER OF THE CRYSTAL DAGGERS

"Wonderful." Marguerite's smile lit up like the sun. "Nora will be so happy. And Ferdy will be glad, too."

"I suppose." My jaw tightened at the mention of my brother-in-law. In one of his rare moments of blunt, unrehearsed honesty, he'd confessed to becoming enchanted with my sister the day we had to sell this particular book. At that memory, a small amount of petty pleasure washed over me; I was happy that I'd found it before he had. "It's something unexpected, that's for sure."

"Can you really expect the unexpected?" Marguerite gave me a flirtatious look.

She was pleased, too, for having pleased me, and her selflessness made me feel even more petty.

"If you've taught me nothing else, it's to be more prepared for life's surprises."

"Surely that's not the only thing I've taught you?" Marguerite gave me a playful wink.

Discretely, I glanced around. We were hidden by the surrounding bookcases, so I leaned forward and brushed a quick kiss across her lips, watching as Marguerite's eyes lit up with pleasure.

The taste of her was minimal and fleeting, but I was both nourished and left wanting more.

Marguerite always enjoyed it when I flirted with her, even if I didn't do it often, especially in public.

She gave me a brilliant smile. "Nora would approve."

"It's not her approval I seek."

"Ah, so it's Ferdy's you look for, then?" Marguerite ran her hands down my cheeks coyishly. "His beard is getting quite thick, too, now that I think of it."

I wrinkled my nose, but didn't say anything in reply as I caught sight of the *Wahabite Jambiya* at my side.

There was no man alive whose approval I sought, but I did want to honor the man who'd given his life and happiness to save my family.

At my sudden sadness, Marguerite laid her lily hand on mine. "My apologies for your pain, *mon amour.*"

"There's no need to apologize." I struggled to keep my tone light. Years of working with Lady Penelope had made Marguerite more intuitive than I would've liked. "Honoring Amir means I must remember him. And … well, he was the closest thing I've had to a father in years," I said softly. "I miss that."

"I know," Marguerite said. "But he is beyond pain now, and I am here to attend to yours."

I frowned. "Lady Penelope didn't assign you to come with me so you could take care of me."

"That is true." Marguerite kept her tone light, too, but underneath her pleasant tone, her patience was dwindling. "But she wouldn't be able to stop me from doing so, either."

There was nothing I could say at her familiar words.

Instead, I glanced around, pretending to look for my stepsister. "Where's Priscilla?"

"Prissy said she would join us at the front of the shop." Marguerite gestured toward the bookcases around us. "She told me she wanted to purchase a few new novels."

I'd never cared for Prissy much, but I was actually glad she had come with us. Once she was established as an apprentice seamstress under Marguerite's sister, Priscilla would have a new home, one free of her pernicious mother. To me, it seemed like an odd, unsavory fate for my long-pampered stepsister, but she was excited to be on her own, and she'd embraced the chance to live in Paris.

THE ORDER OF THE CRYSTAL DAGGERS

"What about your sister?" I asked. "Aren't we supposed to meet her soon?"

"Yes, but not until three o'clock. We have a little time yet." Marguerite gazed outside a nearby window, and I saw the worry in her eyes. "Paris is surprisingly lovely right now, and Madame Phénix's shop is blooming with service, no doubt."

I knew of her past, just as she knew of mine, but neither of us enjoyed discussing such topics if we could avoid it. There were a number of reasons Marguerite had wanted to leave Paris and travel abroad with Lady Penelope.

"Were you worried about coming back here?"

She paused as she pursed her lips. "A little."

"Just a little?" I asked, trying to be gentle.

"I was not sure about the political clime. It has only been a year since Napoleon III died," she murmured noncommittedly. "Lumiere had mentioned how displeased he was over the matter."

"I assumed Lumiere meant that his father would be upset, not that he was himself." I wrinkled my nose at the mention of Lumiere. Ella had a soft spot for that grating, overly self-absorbed degenerate, but at best, I only saw him as an unreliable ally. "Maybe Lumiere was just angry Napoleon was allowed to live after being dethroned. He would see it as a missed opportunity for a good beheading."

"I'm not so sure."

"Well, it is Lumiere we're talking about. Nothing is ever certain when it concerns him."

"True." Marguerite gave me an amused smile. "But he was quite certain that Napoleon was going to shape France's future."

"If he was, it's hard to imagine how it would be better than it is now," I said, gesturing toward the window again.

THE ORDER OF THE CRYSTAL DAGGERS

Outside, the city bustled with energy. After docking at the Port of Paris this morning, we had seen ladies in their bright walking dresses and men sauntering down the streets with hopeful steps. Horses and carriages jostled over the cobblestones, while merchants busily sold their goods. Even common workers seemed full of enthusiasm as we made our way through the shopping district.

"Perhaps you are right," Marguerite said.

"Well, perhaps I'm wrong." I studied the scene before us with new eyes, worried I'd missed something, and that I'd only been too eager to see what was good. "We both know things aren't always what they seem."

"Oh, Ben, please. Harshad and Lady Penelope both said this would be a simple mission."

"If it's just a simple mission, then you should've stayed home."

The instant I spoke the words, I knew I shouldn't have said them at all.

"That's not fair." Marguerite's objection was both swift and full of hurt. "I'm always left at home when you go somewhere."

"It's not like I travel frequently—"

"There was that delivery you made to Brussels two years ago, and you went with Nora to Vienna to report to Franz Joseph, and then you escorted an ambassador to Prussia … " Marguerite counted off my past assignments on her fingers. "Last winter, you were in Berlin for an extra month."

"That one wasn't my fault," I argued. "The snow—"

"That's not my point." Marguerite turned away from me. "You regularly leave me behind. Perhaps you don't realize this, but waiting for you to come home is actually quite tiresome. And though I love your sister, it is vexing to watch her cling to Ferdy so much. I'm convinced he likes having you home since it gives him a break from all her attention."

"I doubt that." I held back a groan, thinking of all the times I'd caught them stealing away to indulge in their passionate embraces. "He's happy to keep her within his reach when I'm home, too."

"Then they're probably happy I'm here so they can be together more." Marguerite crossed her arms over her chest. "Nora's delighted to have her library project, too."

"She would be," I agreed.

Before his death, Amir had mentioned my mother would make notes along the margins of various books as she read. In between her own work for Franz Joseph and the Order, Ella had started going through the manor's library. She'd made slow progress over the years, but considering how slowly I made my own way through *Máma*'s journal, I could understand. There was a trepidation that accompanied the anticipation as we worked, and our reactions ranged from wonder to despair to confusion after all we'd learned about our mother since Lady Penelope and the others had entered our lives.

Thinking of *Máma* reminded me of how sad she'd been when *Otec* would leave. Eventually, she'd had Ella and me to keep her company, but I knew it wasn't enough for her.

I looked down at the book in my hands again and sighed. "I'm sorry for what I said. I am glad you're here with me."

She arched her brow at me, unmoved by my apology, even though it was a rare occurrence between us.

"Please, Marguerite." I bit back a groan. Marguerite was one of the few people with whom I could be vulnerable, but that didn't mean I did it often, and that didn't mean I enjoyed it. "I've lost a lot of people in my life. And I … I can't bear the thought of losing you, too."

THE ORDER OF THE CRYSTAL DAGGERS

"I'm not as frail as you seem to think I am."

"*I* am."

"No, you're not—" Marguerite glanced down at my crooked leg, looking horrified. "I've told you before you're not frail because of your leg."

"No, not that." I stopped myself from rolling my eyes. It was exactly that sort of reason I didn't like to say anything; pity, whether it was my own or someone else's, never did any good. "I'm used to the pain in my leg. I meant I don't like risking your safety or your discomfort."

Marguerite softened. "I can handle the danger and the discomfort."

"I know. But I still don't like it," I grumbled. "And, I don't want to fail the Order, either."

"There's no need to worry about the Order," Marguerite said gently. "Amir and Harshad have taught you well. Lady Penelope has mentioned she would like you to take on more duties."

"I have plenty of duties."

"She'd like you train some new recruits. Lady Penelope and Harshad aren't getting any younger, and you would make a good mentor."

"Well, I don't know about that, but I still don't want to be caught off guard." I paused meaningfully, as she'd just proved my point. "And you do have a way of bringing about the unexpected."

"I do not see you as someone who would step back from a challenge, nor shirk your responsibilities, *mon amour*, even if I am around and making it more difficult for you." Marguerite leaned over and placed a small kiss on my cheek. "If that's all that worries you, then we have nothing to worry about. I trust you, and others do, too."

There was something depressingly familiar about the determined twinkle in her eyes. "Have you been taking lessons on arguing from Lumiere?" I asked.

At my question, she only smirked and pulled away. "Come, now. We have what we were looking for."

The change of subject was sudden enough to let me know we were done arguing, but it was gracious enough that we could both move on. I had a feeling if I was the winner of our disagreement, it was only on Marguerite's terms.

And for now, her terms were acceptable.

I followed closely behind her, keeping the copy of *Morte d'Arthur* secure in my hands.

"Thank you for finding this," I said. "This means a lot to me, and Ella, too."

"And you found it before Ferdy, so that should please you even more." She tossed me a shrewd look over her shoulder. "You know, I'm surprised you don't get along with him better. You're actually quite similar."

"No, we're not," I scoffed. "I wouldn't set out to seduce a naïve girl over a book."

Marguerite laughed. At once, the cheerful sound strengthened both my heart and my resolve. I didn't want her to remain mad at me, even if I understood her anger.

"Well, that's true." Marguerite smiled at me, and I was smiling back as she added, "You prefer to be the one who's seduced."

This time, I didn't bother to ensure we had any privacy; I jerked her back, pulling her against me as I kissed her.

"*Ben.*"

I swallowed her small gasp of surprise, even as she clung to me in that heated, intense moment.

I'd meant to make her fall under my spell, but I only succeeded in falling under hers more deeply. She tasted of springtime and softness, and I found myself wanting not only to fall, but to drown in her essence.

We were both very well kissed before I finally released her.

"I might prefer to be seduced, but I'll participate in a seduction in either role, provided it's with you." I grinned, seeing her eyes glazed over with passion and excitement. "I want you to be safe, Marguerite, but I still want you."

Before she could recover enough to reply, I tucked her arm underneath mine like a proper gentleman, even as other store patrons looked on in disapproval. "Now, let's find Prissy, pay for our purchases, send this book home to Ella, and go meet your family."

2

◊

"Did you see all the books in there? And they had such an adorable little arrangement in their window," Priscilla chattered, as lively as ever while we walked along the Seine River, and even I had to admit it was nice our luggage from the ship would be delivered separately. It was a beautiful day for a walk.

Prissy pointed over to Notre Dame Cathedral. "Oh, look over there! Isn't that just so beautiful? Have you ever seen such a sight?"

"Of course, I have," Marguerite said with a giggle. "I grew up here, after all."

"Oh, that's right! Yes, I nearly forgot."

"Still, Notre Dame is one of the most beautiful places in all the world. I would like to take Ben there one day." Marguerite gave me an eager look, and I didn't resist giving into her silent plea.

"We'll get there soon," I promised. "If that's what you truly want."

"It's all I've ever wanted, *mon amour.*"

"Really?" I was genuinely surprised. When Lady POW had hired her, Marguerite was all too eager to escape Paris. Even now, I didn't think she had any desire to return other than to see her sister.

"Really." Marguerite's smile radiated with joy. "I would have insisted we go there first, but I know you were so happy to visit another bookshop after so many days at sea."

"That's true." I tightened my hand around the book we'd just purchased. Long before Lady Penelope had entered our lives, Ella and I used to plan for Liberté, the name of our own intended bookshop in Prague.

We never did achieve our dream of setting up our own shop, but we both found freedom in other ways.

"How can you be content with just a simple bookshop when we have all of Paris before us?" Priscilla let out a jubilant sigh as Marguerite began to point out other famous places Priscilla had inquired of during our trip, while I studied our surroundings with care.

I was to oversee the signing of the Philastre treaty, but I still wanted to make sure things went smoothly, and that meant I had to research the relationship between the French and the Kingdom of Annam. My progress had been slow as I had to relearn much of the French I'd forgotten over the years.

Tulia would not be pleased.

I smiled a little, thinking back to how she'd taught me and Ella. Tulia had been a hard instructor, rapping my knuckles more than once, and she would have been disappointed at how little I'd remembered from her lessons.

I didn't want to miss her, but sometimes I did.

Tulia was always seemed to know when I was feeling down; she once told me we were alike, since I was crippled with my leg and she was mute and old, but we still did our best to protect Ella from the rest of the world. Tulia had that kind of blunt, unapologetic honesty that was refreshing as much as irritating.

But she was also the one who'd murdered my father, to prevent him from learning of the Order and my mother's participation in it. And when he died, Ella and I had been constantly abused by our stepmother.

Three years later, it was easy to miss the good Tulia brought me, though it was hard to forget the trouble she'd caused.

THE ORDER OF THE CRYSTAL DAGGERS

A foreign voice, just a little way behind us, pulled me out of my thoughts.

"Pardonne, Monsieur? Ou … est … la shoppe de … "

I almost winced at the rough-sounding French. When I looked back, there was a woman standing just a little way from us, talking to a police guard.

I slowed my steps as I looked at the woman. She looked to be close to my age, although it was hard to be sure; she had tan skin, a flat nose, and very large, very brown eyes. She reminded me of both Harshad and Xiana in some ways, and even a little bit like Amir. I was almost certain at the sight of her that she was from the far East, perhaps from the Southeast Asian region, and the longer I saw her, the more I wondered if she'd come with the Annam ambassador. She was dressed in a respectable walking dress, but she seemed unaccustomed to the heavy fabric of the tiered ruffles as she struggled to communicate with the policeman.

"Ben?" Marguerite had noticed my delay. "What is it?"

"She's asking for directions to Madame Phénix's shop," I explained, pointing to the woman. "She looks like she might be a lady from the kingdom of Annam."

Marguerite listened as the lady, who was clearly struggling with the language, attempted to speak in French again.

"Yes," Marguerite agreed. "Poor dear."

Before I could stop her, Marguerite left my side and hurried over to the woman.

"Xin lỗi?"

"Anh có thể giúp em được không?" The woman eyed her warily, and she seemed even more skeptical as Marguerite nodded.

I was about to call for Marguerite to return when the woman's frustration won over her suspicion. She began to speak with Marguerite, and my wife nodded in empathy, and then blinked in surprise.

"What is it, Marguerite?" I looked back at the policeman for help, but found none.

Clearly relieved Marguerite had stepped in to assist the woman, he slouched back from them and walked away, glad it wasn't a matter that required him to act.

"Marguerite?"

Marguerite didn't answer me but continued speaking to the lady and pointing down the streets as she talked.

For some reason, I didn't like how the woman kept glancing around. She didn't seem that interested in Marguerite's assistance.

"Marguerite," I called again, waving at her. "Come back here."

Priscilla stepped up next to me. "Are you in pain, Ben?"

"What?" I frowned. "No. Why?"

"I … I just thought you might have needed her help," Priscilla murmured apologetically. She blushed, and I could only guess that she was recalling all the times her brother, Alex, had made fun of me for my right leg's crooked bend when we were younger. "She's just trying to help the lady. I don't think it'll take that long."

"It's not that." I didn't explain to Priscilla that the woman's lack of interest in Marguerite's help made me uneasy.

The woman then dipped her chin, muttered something that sounded like a goodbye, and waved Marguerite away. Almost glad for her rudeness, I was even more relieved when the woman headed off down a different street from the one my wife had pointed out.

"Wait!" Marguerite called. "That's the wrong way!"

THE ORDER OF THE CRYSTAL DAGGERS

I reached out and took her arm. "Let her go."

"She's not from here, Ben. She doesn't know where to go."

"She was hardly listening to you as you spoke to her."

"She was looking for my sister's shop," Marguerite explained. "I was just about to invite her to join us when she left."

"Do you think we should go after her?" Priscilla asked, clearly unsure of whether she should speak up again.

"That's a good idea," Marguerite began, but I shook my head.

"No," I objected. "Let her go for now."

"We ought to help her," Marguerite pressed. "We are used to being in different cities, Ben. I doubt she is."

"And I doubt she was really interested in your help. You probably shouldn't have said anything in the first place." Marguerite scowled at me, but I stood my ground. "If she does find trouble, she'll be more willing to listen to the next person who offers assistance."

Priscilla shuffled her feet. "Maybe we can just follow after her for a block or two?"

I waited for Marguerite to agree with her and beg me to give in. But instead, she slowly shook her head.

"No. Ben's likely correct. Besides, Hélène is waiting for us. If that woman is looking for her shop, perhaps we will see her soon."

Priscilla bit her lip like she wanted to protest, but as Marguerite and I began walking again, she fell into step beside us.

We were silent as we crossed the Seine River, but once we were on the other side, I pressed a kiss to Marguerite's palm.

"Thank you," I whispered.

THE ORDER OF THE CRYSTAL DAGGERS

"For what?"

"For agreeing with me back there."

She gave me a sidelong look. "You could've been nicer about it, but I do agree with you. The lady was definitely distracted while I was talking with her."

"Is that your way of admitting that I was right?" I teased and brushed up against her lightly.

She rolled her eyes, but she still gave me a smile. "You would be such a good teacher, *mon amour*, if only you were a little more humble. You forget that I was right, too, and Hélène is waiting for us. We are late."

As if to confirm her statement, the bells of Notre Dame rang out, striking three times to mark the hour.

"Where is your sister's shop, Marguerite?" Priscilla asked as we passed by the gardens and turned down onto another street.

I caught a glimpse of the *Palais de Louvre* and the *Palais de la Cité*. Both castles spoke of France's long and rich history and reminded me of *Vyšehrad*, the fortress-castle up the Vltava River back in Bohemia. Further up ahead, I could see the signs for shops, for the *patisseries* and the *boulangeries*, a milliner's shop and flower stations optimally positioned for sales.

"It's not too much further," Marguerite answered. "Hélène works by the Latin Quarter, just off the main strip."

"Madame Phénix, you mean."

Marguerite chuckled. "Hélène can change her name all she'd like, but she's still my sister, no matter how famous she is."

"The name is part of the reason she's so famous, no doubt," I said.

THE ORDER OF THE CRYSTAL DAGGERS

A modiste as famous and financially successful as Hélène would need a reputation for exclusive and upscale services. The name and persona she'd established had lent that illusion long enough for it to become a reality.

"Yes," Marguerite agreed, but the cheerfulness in her voice instantly faded. "She learned that much from our mother."

Marguerite and Hélène were the illegitimate offspring of the owner of *Salon Angelique*, a prestigious Parisian brothel, and her unnamed lover. The two girls had been raised to take over the brothel one day, but when their mother unexpectedly died, Marguerite and Hélène discovered the true, dire state of their finances. Faced with the possibility of losing their home, Marguerite suggested using their patrons as sources of information and blackmail. Her idea worked, and although their financial situation improved, money was not enough to lift their spirits. Marguerite sank into a deep melancholy, while Hélène poured all her anxiety and extra energy into designing clothes. Soon after that, Lady Penelope met them while on an assignment in Paris. Thanks to Marguerite and Hélène's illicit information, my grandmother completed her mission. As a gesture of gratitude, Lady POW became their principal investor in a new business venture. *Salon Angelique* burned to the ground, and Madame Phénix's shop made its grand opening. For all her hardness towards others, Lady POW still had a soft heart, no matter how much Ella said otherwise, as her treatment of Hélène and Marguerite proved.

I reached over and took hold of my wife's hand, reassuring her without words her past didn't affect how I felt about her.

"*Arrêtez, voleur!*"

At the angry shout, I blinked, suddenly aware of footsteps pounding behind me. I glanced around, looking for what was wrong—only to spy a swiftly moving shadow making its way through the crowd.

The strained voice full of authority and anger called out again. "*Larron!*"

"'*Thief*.'" Marguerite's eyes went wide as she translated the yelling.

But I was already moving. "Get over," I ordered, pushing Marguerite off to the side.

The shadow darted around and slipped through the crowd with expert grace. I caught a brief glimpse of a distinctively male face under a bowler hat, then positioned myself in his path.

Just as he moved to avoid me, I stepped into him.

We collided, hard and fast, forcefully propelling us to the ground. He was a short, young man, likely only a few years younger than I. He wore the clothes of a street urchin, but dealing with Ferdy had taught me to take a closer look, which vindicated my suspicions. Under his ragged collar, the bright white of a proper shirt peeked out, and his shoes were in good condition, even if I didn't recognize the design. His skin tone was similar to the woman Marguerite had tried to help earlier, and he had straight, black hair. His broad, flat nose was covered in blood. The bowler hat might have hidden his face, but there was no mistaking his anger as he glared at me.

He'd been caught off guard by my movement as I was by the pain, but thanks to speed and youth on his part and training on mine, we recovered quickly.

Marguerite called for me, but I ignored her.

"*Arrêtez!*" The voice from earlier filled the street, and seconds later, a familiar-looking policemen came around the corner.

"*Ngu thê!*" The apparent thief, still bleeding, yelled at me, no doubt cursing me in his native language, but, as he brushed away the blood on his face, I saw what the policeman was after.

THE ORDER OF THE CRYSTAL DAGGERS

A large, bulky package was strapped to his back, a small case that didn't fit with the rest of his outfit; I grabbed for it, but it was tied around the thief's shoulders.

The rope around the package snapped, further infuriating the thief.

"*Mày khùng tới nơi,*" he shouted as he tried to swat me away, but I didn't let go.

Out of the corner of my eye, I could see the policeman approach. I tightened my hold on the case, determined to keep the thief from break away. If he couldn't leave, he would be arrested.

I was just feeling victorious, when all of a sudden, he let go.

Immediately, I went flying backward, lost my balance, and dropped the case in surprise.

The thief didn't waste his time. He snatched up the box again and sneered. I braced for another attack, but he merely tossed his hat at me as I sat on the ground.

The policeman cut through the crowd just as I stood up.

"*Arrêtez-vous,*" he yelled, grabbing my shoulder. "*Larron!*"

"No, wait. It's not him you're after," Marguerite cried out.

Dealing with a street thief was not part of my job for the Order. I could let him go and let the police handle it.

But I wouldn't.

"Marguerite, stay with Prissy," I ordered, scrambling out of the policeman's reach. "I'll meet up with you later."

"Ben!"

I glanced over my shoulder just as Marguerite stepped forward and blocked the policeman from grabbing me a second time. As she explained the situation and he argued back, I slipped away, following after the real thief.

Pushing Marguerite's worried voice out of my head, I ran down the street and turned the corner into an alleyway. My right leg was still weak, and the rest of my body was still stinging from its earlier impact, but I pressed on.

I would not let my pain get the best of me—not when I had a job to do.

THE ORDER OF THE CRYSTAL DAGGERS

3

◊

By the time the thief reached the end of the block, he'd noticed I was following him. No doubt I was hard to miss; due to my leg, I limped as I ran, even if it was a little less noticeable than when I walked.

I saw him glance behind himself more than a few times, watching as I followed after him. His curiosity allowed me to advance on his lead, and even with the limp, I knew it would be only a matter of time before I caught up with him.

But as I turned the corner at the second block, I quickly skidded to a halt.

A large vase flew through the air toward me.

I barely managed to dodge it. Jumping to the side, I used my good leg and arm to ricochet off a nearby wall, and the vase smashed to the ground and broke into shards.

Regaining my footing, I resumed the chase, drawing even with a flower saleslady who was yelling and throwing pots at the thief. If he'd stolen the vase from her, she was understandably upset.

Inspired, I grabbed a pot myself and took careful aim.

Crash!

I smiled a little as the pot smashed right on top of his head, and he pitched forward onto the ground.

The saleslady grinned at me, clearly grateful and amused, but in the blink of an eye, the thief got up, scowled at us, and then resumed his running.

At that point, there was no doubt in my mind that he was younger than I. It was obvious in the way he sped through the streets, practically dancing between pedestrians and weaving his way between wagons and carriages, and in how he could keep going whatever other obstacles were in his way. Reluctantly, I admired how he seemed just as agile with his mind as he was with his feet. And then I ran after him again, too.

My discomfort increased with each step. I was running out of strength, but despite the pain, I pressed forward, forcing myself to run even faster.

He slithered up to a hackney, only to steal a cloak from the carriage box and wrap it around himself. Twisting the collar to hide his face, he walked away at a normal pace, trying to melt into the crowd.

I paused and pretended to look around, confused and lost, letting him think he'd tricked me. My ruse gave me a moment to catch my breath and steady myself, and it gave him the chance to make a mistake.

Out of the corner of my eye, I watched as a Parisian man hailed the thief and asked him for a ride, believing him to be the carriage driver.

It was then, while he was distracted by the man's request, that I leaped at him.

"I can still see your shoes," I yelled as I tackled him. "I know you're the thief!"

He shouted back at me in his native language, but even if I didn't know what he was saying, at least the people around us would know what was happening.

The cloak twitched and fell, revealing his face. Clearly, he'd been caught, and he'd been caught off guard, too.

Before I could celebrate, he slid out of the cloak, leaving the material in my hand even as he slipped from my grasp and rolled away.

My mouth dropped open in surprise. I was even more disgruntled, however, when the cloak caught on his bag, and I was jerked off to the side.

I still held onto the cloak, while he tried to free the package from the material. Quickly, I pulled out my *Wahabite Jambiya* and slashed through the cloth, cutting the bulky package from its belt. He went flying backward.

There was a sickening *crunch* as his head slammed into the ground, and he lay very still.

"Oh, great," I muttered while I sheathed my blade, hoping I wouldn't be arrested for murder as well as burglary.

I let go of the cloak and the package and carefully pushed myself up. I could feel the stinging shadow of bitter work, but I wanted to make sure he was still alive.

His eyes were closed and his jaw was slack, but I felt a pulse at his neck and his breathing was there, even if it seemed shallow.

Relieved, I sat for a moment, catching my breath, and tried to remember what I'd learned about treating injuries. Marguerite had tried to teach me what she'd learned under Amir, and I had great respect for her skills, especially when it was my own pain she tended. Nothing helpful came to mind. I sighed.

"You've caused me quite a bit of trouble today," I muttered to the young man.

Carefully and reluctantly, I hoisted him off the ground and placed him on my shoulders. He was shorter than I, but young and muscular. Gritting my teeth, I resolved to carry him, no matter how long it took or how heavy he was, but his leg twitched.

He jolted, rocking my balance again, and pushed himself from my shoulders. He grabbed at his head and groaned in pain, before covering his eyes with his hands.

THE ORDER OF THE CRYSTAL DAGGERS

"Are you hurt?" I asked carefully. "I mean, very badly?"

His eyes peeked at me through his fingers.

And then he lunged forward, kneed me in the gut, and threw me down to the ground.

I yelped as I landed hard on my back. He was already running as I pulled myself up into a sitting position.

But this time, he didn't take his bag with him.

He'd left it on the ground, just a few feet from me.

"Well, at least there's that," I muttered, picking myself up off the street and brushing myself off. My whole body screamed at me, angry and in agony.

"Ben!"

I turned around to see Marguerite. She was running toward me, holding up her skirts, concern etched into her lovely features. She stopped just shy of embracing me, and I was relieved. I doubt I could have withstood the pressure of her embrace, and we already had an audience.

"What happened? Are you all right?" Marguerite looked me over as carefully as she could in public.

"I'm fine," I replied, shooing her back. "I didn't catch him."

"Can you walk still?" Marguerite leaned over and placed my arm on her shoulder.

"I'm fine." I was lying, but only a little. "Anyway, where is Prissy? You didn't leave her with the policeman, did you?"

"She was right behind me a moment ago." Marguerite squinted down the lane, and then pointed. "There she is. She's coming."

"I told you to stay with her," I muttered. "Not drag her here."

"The policeman wanted to know more about you," Marguerite said. "So, I thought it was best to leave. And I didn't want you to come back to deal with him. He insisted that you were the real guilty one, although I'll never understand why."

"I can guess." The policeman been only too happy to let Marguerite take care of the foreign lady before; with my limp, I was willing to gamble that he thought I'd be the easier one to catch.

"Oh, Ben." Marguerite softened as she realized what I'd meant, but I bristled.

"I don't want or need your pity," I grumbled. "As you well know. Or you should, after all these years."

"I have no pity for you, *mon amour.* You are not a victim." Marguerite scowled back at me, her indignation a rebuke. She had always tended to me in genuine care, not sympathy, and we both knew it. "If I do have any pity, it's for him, if that's what he truly thinks. And if I have anything, it's contempt for your poor logic in this case than anything else."

"*My* poor logic? What are you talking about? I already know I didn't have to go after the thief."

"It's not that you chased him," Marguerite argued. "It's that you left me and Prissy behind."

"I couldn't wait for you both." I gestured back toward the top of the street, where Prissy was still making her way toward us. "Not if I was going to catch him."

"You said you'd meet up with us later. But you don't know where my sister's shop is, and you could've gotten lost."

"Even if I did get lost," I said, "I know how to retrace my steps."

"And by the time you did that, Prissy and I would've been arrested ourselves."

I arched my brow. "I doubt that."

"Well, we weren't, because we came after you," Marguerite insisted. "And I knew you wouldn't want me to get into any trouble."

"I would've preferred you waited."

She gave me an overly sweet smile. "I didn't know how long you would take."

"Ben! Marguerite! Oh, thank goodness I found you."

Marguerite and I went silent as Prissy finally joined us. There was no point in arguing over what should have or could have happened, and we both knew it.

"Did you catch him, Ben?" Prissy asked. She was panting hard, but she looked at both of us in eager expectation.

I almost groaned. I didn't need her obsessing over any part of my mission, or even any side events I chose to undertake. It was bad enough Marguerite wanted to do more; I didn't need Prissy acting up, too.

Instead, I only shook my head. "No, I didn't catch him. But I did get him to drop the case he was carrying. So at least we'll be able to return whatever he stole." I walked over to the case and picked it up; it looked heavy, but it was much lighter than I'd anticipated. "I wonder what it is."

"Let's take it to Hélène's," Marguerite suggested. "We'll have more room to better examine it there."

"Yes." I nodded, already hauling the thief's case onto my back. "But I'll return it myself. I don't want either of you to worry about it."

"But we might be able to help," Marguerite said.

I shook my head. "Not now, please. We can discuss it later, if you like."

THE ORDER OF THE CRYSTAL DAGGERS

The barest hint of a pout appeared on Marguerite's face, but she said nothing.

She had come with me to Paris because of her sister. She was not working for the Order, as I was. I did not want her to get into any more trouble, and I didn't want her to think she ought to join me on more of my missions in the future.

"Come," I said, hoping to cheer her up some. "Hélène is waiting for us."

4

◊

We were just about to enter Hélène's shop near the Latin Quarter when its door burst open and a woman who was undeniably related to Marguerite appeared in our path. She was nearly identical to her sister, with delicate hands and the same blunt nose, kind smile, and sharp emerald eyes. She wore a dress of several bright, jewel-tone colors, and her own mop of curly hair was braided and hung down her back.

"Marguerite! You're here." She opened her arms wide as she embraced Marguerite. "I have been waiting all day for your arrival."

"Hélène." Marguerite's smile was warm. "It's so good to see you again. It has been too long."

Hélène pulled back from her and glanced over at me. "It has been too long for certain. But at least I can see for myself my baby sister is in good hands."

"Very good hands." Marguerite gave me a flirtatious look as Hélène continued to scrutinize me.

"It is lovely to formally meet you, Miss Hélène," I said, taking her hand and bowing over it gallantly. It was no small feat, with my leg in pain and the thief's large package hanging over my shoulder, but I could see her appreciation for my effort.

Hélène curtsied back. "I do regret I wasn't able to make it to the wedding," she said apologetically. "But to be fair, I should have had better notice."

I said nothing to that; I had offered to Marguerite to wait to get married, letting her invite others and pull a reception and a wedding together. She didn't like the idea of waiting long, even if it was just until traveling was easier, and when my friends from The Cabal, Clavan, Eliezer, and Jarl, all set up a small reception for us, neither of us could say no.

Neither of us wanted to, either.

We were married a few short weeks after Lady Penelope had given us her permission and blessing, and that was all I really wanted before we were wed. I didn't need her approval, but I felt it was honorable and right to ask for it; she was my grandmother, after all. Still, I doubted she was excited to see the news of our nuptials so soon.

Marguerite finished introducing Prissy to Hélène, and they were all talking excitedly when I heard a small scrape behind us.

I looked around, narrowing my eyes.

I couldn't explain it, but I suddenly felt as though we were being watched.

Is the thief back? Did he follow us?

"Oh, listen to me just chatting incessantly. Come on in," Hélène insisted, pulling on my sleeve. "You will not believe what I have for you. I've been working on some really special projects of late, and I just must show them off."

Before I knew it, we were pushed through the doorway and thrust into an entirely new world. There were piles of cloth on shelves and chairs; large mirrors were placed behind tall privacy screens, and everywhere I looked, it was clean and shining. There were even some gowns hanging up, each one more elaborate than the last.

"Your shop is so lovely," Prissy said shyly, blushing a little. "I don't know if my work will be good enough for you."

"My seamstresses and I will get you there," Hélène promised her. "Now, don't worry about that. Instead, look here. I designed it for you to wear tomorrow."

She reached out for a gown. I liked the look of it; a claret-colored gown would look wonderful on my wife. But I was confused when Hélène grabbed the skirts and pulled them out.

"Oh, wow," Marguerite said. "That's amazing, Hélène."

"What is it?" I didn't see anything but a skirt.

"She's added another layer into it, so there are shadow pockets," Marguerite explained. She stood up and pulled the fabric a little tighter, and I could see the folds a little more clearly; they were perfectly placed for collecting small objects and hiding them discreetly. "This is brilliant."

"What's it for?" I asked, still confused.

"What's it for? Why, what else? It's for espionage," Hélène said with a small laugh. "Come on, *mon frère*, don't tell me you didn't think I would want to help you and Marguerite on your job."

I'd hoped to discourage Marguerite from accompanying me on my future missions.

I thought visiting with her sister would offer her a nice, happy distraction while I figured out what to do with the thief and his mystery case and still make it to the treaty signing.

Unfortunately, I suspected Hélène did not share in my hopes.

"We're just going to the Philastre treaty signing," I said uneasily. "Lady Penelope only wanted us to observe and suggest policies for the Order regarding the Kingdom of Annam and Far East."

"Come now, what's wrong with a well-armored attire, even if it's a gown?"

"Nora would love to see some of these, too," Marguerite reminded me, as she and Prissy began looking over the other dresses.

The two of them fawned over the different items Hélène had prepared. There was a bonnet that carried hair pins and lock picks, a feathered fan that concealed daggers, and even a reticule that could easily hold a revolver and some extra bullets.

As I watched them, my uneasiness grew. I loved my wife; I loved her smile, her laugh, and even her gentle stubbornness. I loved the two of us, and how we were together, and I loved how she loved me.

I did not want trouble between us.

Hélène was a clever woman, and one just as beautiful as her sister, she could be a bad influence on Marguerite—and that worried me.

"There's more in the back," Hélène said. "I even have a walking stick that conceals a rapier for you, Benedict, and I just finished up a design for a tall hat, just like the one Mr. Lincoln used to wear. I heard he liked to use it so he could keep his notes nearby. Isn't that so thoughtful? I'm trying to figure out how to make sure nothing falls when the hat is pulled off, but I daresay it'll be a great asset to you once I'm finished with it."

"Ben might be able to help you," Marguerite said. "He's great with designs like that."

I felt a little embarrassed as Marguerite listed off several examples of my technical skills, including my leg brace, my lock picks, and even some of the ways I'd worked on concealing my own weapons as I traveled.

"If you don't mind, I'd like to wait on things like that. Right now, we have a bit of a mystery to solve," I said, grabbing the thief's case. I held it up to show her. "I'd like to see what's inside this package."

"Is that not your luggage?" Hélène frowned. "Perhaps I should check with my housekeeper. Mrs. DeSaille had mentioned that your luggage had arrived earlier, but she was supposed to see to your rooms."

"This isn't mine," I explained.

"Oh, yes," Marguerite said. "Hélène, you won't believe what happened to us on our way here."

Hélène handed me a pair of shears as Marguerite and Prissy took turns telling her the tale of my heroism and noble quest to stop the passing thief. I almost rolled my eyes at their exaggerations, but I knew their account was one of goodwill, so I said nothing.

"Ben didn't have to step in at all, either," Marguerite said with a beaming smile. "But he still recovered the package."

"And the police officer didn't arrest him," Prissy added.

"I see." Hélène watched me as I cut the rest of the rope away from the case. "Well, it's good to know that some true gentlemen are still out there, *n'est-pas*? To think, you must be the most noble man I've ever met. No wonder Margie decided to marry you, Benedict."

Her words were hardened, but not with malice, and I remembered that Hélène had been a prostitute in *Salon Angelique* longer than her sister, before my grandmother had intervened and burned down their past.

So instead of engaging with her bitterness, I simply looked up. "Margie?" I repeated innocently.

Marguerite giggled. "You know she means me, Ben."

"I know, but I thought it was a silly name for you." I turned back to the case, opening it up. "Well, look at this."

Inside the thief's package was a folded canvas. Even without unfolding it, I knew it was a large one, taller than me and much wider, too.

"It's a painting," Marguerite said. "Prissy, will you help us?"

"Certainly."

Together, we gently unfolded it. It was old, and there was something familiar about it, too. A half-nude woman warrior held up a large French flag. Several bodies lay on the ground, and fighting raged while the woman led men into battle.

"*Mon Dieu.*" Hélène gasped. Her hand covered her open mouth in shock. "It's Marianne—Lady Liberty herself."

"Who is she?" Prissy asked, looking the woman over carefully.

"She is the spirit of the French people," Hélène explained quickly. "This is simply amazing. This painting is a legendary piece of artwork. It was supposedly destroyed in 1855, after it caused a stir at a Salon. The artist himself, the great painter, Delacroix, said it was best hidden away from all of history, given what rebellion and revolution has done to our country."

"If it was supposed to be destroyed, how did a regular thief acquire it?" Prissy asked.

"I doubt he was a regular thief," I murmured, recalling the determined look on the young man's face. "But I'm not sure we'll be able to find him again."

"If he's looking for this painting, perhaps we will see him again," Marguerite said.

"In the meantime, at least I know where to return it," I said. "I can take it to a museum. They should know how to take care of such a painting."

I looked around for agreement, and all of them seemed to think that was the right course to take. I felt much better, even if I was uneasy about having such a rare artifact on hand.

"Perhaps I should take it over now." I motioned to Prissy and Marguerite, and they began to help me fold it back up, as it had been in the case.

"*Non*, not now," Hélène said. "You have only just arrived. There is no need to rush right now, is there?"

"No, there's not." Marguerite looked at me with pleading eyes.

"It would be just a quick trip," I said, keeping my tone light.

"Would it? I doubt that," Marguerite said. "What if the police comes back for you? And who knows how long it will take you to find a museum curator at this hour?"

"She is right," Hélène agreed. "The *Palais de Louvre* is the best option for such a place, and their art exhibitions will be closed to the public soon."

"I could take it to a Salon," I suggested. "That's probably where it came from, right? It seems fitting for it to have been in a smaller place, with hidden or rare paintings like these that are only open to a high-paying or select audience."

"Ben, let's just save it for tomorrow," Marguerite begged. "We have the signing tomorrow, after all, and we don't want to miss that. That's the whole reason we came."

"*Excusez-moi?*" Hélène lifted her brow and crossed her arms. "Am I nothing, then?"

"No, of course not," Prissy said. "I had to come and see you, too. And Marguerite has been talking of little else but you and Paris since we left Prague."

As they began to argue, I could only sigh.

"I'll hold off on dealing with this with tomorrow, if that is your wish," I said, speaking loudly enough to overrun their conversation. "I don't like the idea of it being here, though. I wasn't able to catch the thief."

"It'll be fine for one day," Hélène said. "I have my own guards positioned around the shop if needed."

"You do?" Prissy's eyes went wide. Why?"

Hélène gave Prissy a generic reply, saying as one of Paris' most famous modistes, she had a duty to keep her high-paying clients safe as well as her own person, but I knew the real reason; Hélène and Marguerite had a past, and it was a dangerous one.

I relaxed a little. Hélène was telling the truth, and that was likely why I'd felt like we were being watched earlier; we probably were, but there was no reason to think we were being watched by the young thief.

"Ben?"

Marguerite glanced over at me, and we exchanged a look.

And then I put the canvas back inside the case and secured the ties again. "You asked me to leave it until tomorrow," I said. "Very well. Tonight is for our family."

Hélène looked pleased, and Prissy smiled, and Marguerite's eyes glistened with delight.

"Thank you, *mon amour*," Marguerite whispered.

"Well, I think it's time we reacquainted ourselves, my baby sister." Hélène clapped her hands, and her housekeeper, an older lady named Mrs. DeSaille, appeared in the doorway. "Let's go to the parlor for tea, shall we? Oh, and I'll give you a tour of the shop and my rooms upstairs. I did get your rooms all nice and ready to go for you tonight. And there's more! While I must work some while you're here, I do promise, I will take you on a tour of Paris you will never forget. There's just so much to do, and so much for you to see. So much has changed since you've been here last … "

Hélène was still prattling on as Marguerite and I reached for each other. I took her hand in mine, and she tightened her grip on me.

"Thank you," she whispered again, pressing a quick kiss onto my cheek. "This means a lot to me."

THE ORDER OF THE CRYSTAL DAGGERS

"I know."

I said nothing else as we fell into step behind Hélène and Prissy; but, really, what else was there that could I say?

Marguerite was likely right that it would take a longer time than we would both like for me to return the painting, and we didn't have much time before Lady Penelope would send us back to Prague. I could wait for now. And it was something Marguerite had asked of me. I couldn't say no to her, not when it was unreasonable to do so.

THE ORDER OF THE CRYSTAL DAGGERS

5

◊

Whether it was from our prolonged walk through Paris, the several previous days at sea, or just the general exhaustion that came with traveling, I was more than grateful when Marguerite was finally ready to retire for the night. For hours, we had talked with Hélène about her business, the gossip around the city, and the various rumors of war and intrigue surrounding the world.

When I was growing up, after *Máma* passed, I'd wondered why *Otec* had never bothered to go out much. He would travel frequently, as I did, but he always came home and read through his books or kept busy with his work. As an ambassador for the king, there was plenty he had to do. He would further check on our farmland and the small cluster of animals we kept, and there were always accounts to balance. When he married Cecilia, my first thought was he'd done so in order to have help with running our household.

Hélène's rooms above her shop were elegant, if cluttered. Prissy wasn't the only seamstress staying with her, though. Several other apprentices—young girls who looked as if Hélène had brought them in off the street—would not look me in the eye as Hélène introduced them to us. Prissy went with them and Mrs. DeSaille, the housekeeper, to get settled in her room, but Marguerite and I had a room just down the hall from Hélène's quarters.

Marguerite tripped. I grabbed hold of her, steadying her as we walked toward our room.

"You probably shouldn't have had the champagne," I told her.

She giggled. "I don't drink it very often. And Hélène wanted to toast our wedding. That was kind of her. You didn't have to make her feel awkward by refusing it."

"And you didn't have to try to make her feel better by drinking my share." I raised a brow. "You know I'm not fond of champagne. If I'm going to drink, I prefer brandy. It dulls the pain in my leg."

"But it also dulls your mind." Marguerite nodded. "And you don't want to worry about that."

"Yes."

"You have other things to worry about."

"Yes." I looked at her pointedly. "I do."

She sighed. "You don't have to worry about me so much, you know. It's so very tiresome, Ben."

"My concern for you is not turned off and on at your whim, Madame. That's not how it works."

"It's not a matter of working or not," she replied. "It's a matter of trust, between us, and a matter of faith, should things go awry."

I said nothing. Instead, I opened the door to the room and found everything in order. The curtains were pulled back, and from where we were, the city shone like the night sky. There were streets of lights, all of them twinkling and sparkling, as the darkness settled in around it.

"Paris suits you," I told Marguerite, as she came to stand beside me. "It's playful, energetic, and much … softer, I would say. Prague always felt stilted to me. Ella says she sees the city as a fairy tale, but this place is more like a dream."

"I have enjoyed forgetting Paris," Marguerite admitted. "If only because it means I get to experience it anew this time. I did not see much that has changed since I was last here; but I can almost feel the difference. The people here now are more hopeful for the future."

"Well, no wonder it suits you, then," I said, pressing a kiss to her forehead. "That's how I feel when you're around."

She pouted. "I wouldn't know it, seeing how often you seem to wish I wasn't."

A new wave of weariness washed over me. "What of when we have children, Marguerite?" I asked. "What will you do then?"

"Yes, Ben, what of when we have children?" Marguerite looked back at me with calculated consideration. "Would you prefer to leave them at home with me and keep them from knowing their legacy, as you were?"

"I'd rather have that, than thrust them into something they're not prepared for, as you were."

I'm not sure why she was shocked at my reply; her own jab was just as stinging.

I loved Marguerite, and really, I did not want to hurt her. I knew, in bringing up her own mother's legacy, I was only anxious for her to see reason.

"I already know better than my mother did," Marguerite said slowly, her voice edged with bitterness, even as she seemed resigned. "And you ought to know better than yours, too."

I crossed my arms over my chest. "I do."

"Well, then let us prove we're both better than our parents."

"We're already better than our parents." I gestured out the window. "We're married, we're together, and we know all of each other's secrets."

Marguerite bit her lip. "I suppose that's mostly true."

"Mostly?"

"Never mind." Marguerite shrugged. "I meant we ought to work out a compromise. It seems reasonable to say that we'll likely have some more disagreements over the years."

"I'd rather not."

"Of course we will, Ben. You don't want a wife who will blindly follow you."

"Oh, you mean I don't?" I gave her a teasing smile.

"No." She put her arms around my neck. "You want one who will challenge you and fight to be by your side in all things."

"I guess it's fair to say we've had our share of challenges." I put my hands on her hips and she stepped closer into me. "Honestly, if Lady POW is not enough to scare you away from me, surely our fights won't, either."

She gave me a playful smile. "Even when I'm arguing with you over the Order's missions?"

"Even then," I agreed, grinning. "Especially since I win those arguments."

"You do not," Marguerite objected. "I just let you think you do."

"Fortunately for us, there are ways we can both win," I said, as I pulled her close and finally kissed her again.

Marguerite could only murmur in agreement as we pressed closer to each other. The earlier rush I'd felt in kissing her came back, more potent and captivating than ever. Marguerite made love the same way she loved me; she tenderly massaged away my pains as she stirred my heart to life. I responded with passion and desperation, eager to impress myself upon her.

It was hard to believe there was ever a time I didn't need her as ardently as I did now.

When we'd first met, Marguerite had been quick to flirt with me—something I disdained initially. I didn't need her sympathy, fake or otherwise, and I told her so, in no uncertain terms.

She surprised me by readily agreeing with me.

"Everyone pities a victim, but a man who overcomes his pain and fights injustice is to be admired." She remained steadfast and held her ground. "And I do not believe you are a victim."

Considering how angry, bitter, and impolite I'd been to her up until that point, I had to respect her for dealing with my churlishness with aplomb. She could have easily slapped me for my rudeness and I wouldn't have blamed her for doing so. Instead, she excused herself and left me standing there, dumbstruck and dumbfounded, just staring after her.

After that, I started to like her.

Our stolen glances soon turned into stolen moments, and our stolen moments soon gave way to stolen kisses.

I would look for her after my training sessions, and even Ella's despair during the winter of our first mission wasn't enough to keep me from looking for Marguerite.

When we had the chance, we would talk about everything from our favorite books and hobbies to our pasts and even some of our secrets; I remembered the moments where I would just watch her speak, feeling as though every word was an antidote to the old pains in my heart. She was a little older than me, but both of us had experienced profound suffering, and it was a revelation to find my company was just as healing to her as hers was to me.

But then my leg broke for the second time on the *Salacia*, and I discovered Lady POW had instructed her to see to my care—even my *intimate* care, if needed. Angry and betrayed, I confronted Marguerite about it.

THE ORDER OF THE CRYSTAL DAGGERS

I crumpled when she did not deny her orders.

Just as I intended to turn her away for good, Marguerite, in a rare moment of anger, refused to let me push her away. She insisted Lady Penelope wouldn't be able to order her away from me and then declared she was in love with me.

After my shock wore off, I told Marguerite she sounded ridiculous, and she agreed with me.

Our stolen kisses reverted back to stolen glances, but even during our confrontation, I knew it was too late; she had managed to steal my heart, too.

The happiest moment of my life was when Lady Penelope reluctantly agreed to our marriage. I never felt more alive than when I had Marguerite with me.

"Ben."

Marguerite murmured my name as she lay down on my shoulder, and I held onto her.

The last thing I saw before my eyes closed to sleep was her lovely face, framed by her sprawled-out curls.

By the time the morning light crept in, she was on her own side of our bed, curled into the soft covers, as cozy as a kitten.

I watched her for a few moments, awed at the feeling of perfect contentedness I felt.

When Ella and I had been younger, and our parents were gone, she'd promised that I was all the family she needed. I'd told her she would feel differently one day, and she had told me I'd given up on the prospect of having a wife too early. It turned out we were both right about each other; even if I'd felt more than a little rebuffed when Ferdy wedged his way into our family, I could not imagine my life without Marguerite.

And I was more than blessed, too, to have a wife who not only loved me, but she didn't mind how I made a living—in fact, she was eager to join me in my work at every opportunity.

"Marguerite?" I whispered, tucking a loose curl behind her ear. "Are you awake?"

She shook her head and buried her face into the covers. I smiled; it seemed I wasn't the only one who was tired from our recent ventures. When her breathing returned to its steady rhythm, I decided to let her sleep.

She had come to spend some time with Hélène, and I would let her attend to her family while I took care of my mission.

I got up and moved as silently as I could, wincing at the pain in my crooked leg. All the running had been far from kind to it, but I would recover. It would just take time.

I was nearly out the door when I heard Hélène's voice from behind me.

"Does my sister know you're leaving?"

I turned around. Hélène was wearing a morning dress, and her hair was loose; she was clearly comfortable being the queen in her own quarters, even with guests present. She had a teacup and a saucer in her hand as she stood by the parlor door.

"Marguerite knows I have work here," I replied neutrally. "I told you about the treaty signing last night."

"Yes, yes, I know," Hélène smiled and waved her hand, as if to dismiss her concerns. "Lady Penelope is a fine patron, and I would not want to disappoint her. I am glad to see that our late hours did not keep you down."

I noticed she did not say anything about Marguerite, and I gave her a polite nod.

Perhaps we were not as opposed to each other's ideals as I'd thought.

"Please let her rest," I said. "She's had a hard night."

"So I have heard, *mon frère*. But not to worry. Hard nights can be enjoyable in their own way." Hélène gave me a smirk as she stirred her tea.

She pretended to ignore me as I blushed.

"Thank you," I muttered back. "I'll be back later. Excuse me."

"Enjoy the ceremony," Hélène replied. "This is the second treaty we've had with Annam, is it not? Perhaps we'll have a third, even. But given our history, it'll still be a decade before it comes around again."

"Let's hope it'll be the last, and this one will work."

"Hope? Yes. Trust? No." Hélène gave me another smirk. "But that's good for you, if it fails, *n'est-pas?* Repeat business."

"There's no need to hope for a repeat of unpleasant business."

Hélène gave me an approving look. "I can see why my sister loves you. You are a man of honor first, and then a man of action."

"I'd hardly call myself a man of action."

"Well, that's another noble trait of yours. Humility." Hélène looked me over. "Combine that with your honor and integrity, and I assume your reliability, and that is all my sister and I have ever wanted in a man."

I frowned a little, frustrated at her goading. I didn't know why she would say such a thing or what her point was in doing so. Was she trying to test me?

THE ORDER OF THE CRYSTAL DAGGERS

She cocked her head to the side a little. "Did it bother you to learn of her past? There is plenty of scandal in both our lives."

"Marguerite is my wife," I answered, more than a little irritated. I also knew Marguerite herself would be appalled and embarrassed by Hélène's remarks. "I'm more concerned with her future than her past."

"What about her heritage?" Hélène pressed.

"What's wrong with her heritage?"

"So you don't know?" She bit her lip, much as Marguerite had done the night before.

"Marguerite told me about your mother, and her Salon," I said. "If that's what you mean."

Hélène shrugged, and then laughed a bit. "Never mind," she said, waving her hand and brushing the matter aside. "I was more interested to see if you indeed had any flaws at all. But I guess not, *n'est-pas?*"

"I'm sure Marguerite will tell you I have plenty, especially if you wait until after I give her orders to follow."

I turned to walk away, but as I glanced back, I was surprised to see Hélène looked glum.

"What is it?" I asked, frowning. "Do you have a problem with me, Hélène? I'd rather things be plain between us. We are adults; we can still maintain pleasantries in public, and you don't need to worry about Marguerite."

"Oh, I don't worry for her," Hélène said. "She has you. Rather, I'm quite jealous."

"Jealous?"

"Yes," Hélène said with a sigh. "I imagine it's not very likely there will be another such a man as yourself out there for me. Marguerite is truly a lucky woman to have found you."

Hélène had a prosperous career and she lived in Paris, a city with everything she could ever need, no more than a few blocks away. And she had come a long way from her roots and made a respectable life for herself.

I could say nothing to that. Instead, I merely bowed my head to her again in farewell. "I must be going. Good day, Hélène."

She waved, and despite her clear bitterness, she smiled at me. "Good day, Ben."

6

◊

By the time I arrived at the *Palais du Luxembourg,* I was grateful to be alone and back to work. Hélène's morning conversation had been strangely unsettling, and I was glad to have a distraction.

Even though it was a relatively short walk from the Latin Quarter, I hailed a carriage. Dirtying my formal suit dirty by walking would not leave a good impression, and a carriage ride would allow me to use the time to go over the notes I'd made over the last few weeks.

When I walked through the palace entrance, I regretted leaving Marguerite behind. I knew enough French to get by, though, and the one benefit of listening to Hélène and Marguerite talk for hours last night was that I was better able to listen and understand French by the time we retired. But learning a new language required extensive practice, and I would need more to master it yet.

As I jumped down from the carriage, plenty of people had already gathered outside the palace. The small crowd milled around, hoping to get a glimpse of history in the making. A wave of whispers suddenly shot through the crowd, and I turned to see where everyone's attention had shifted.

Coming down the street was a large litter bearing a small, ornately decorated chair, half-covered by a silk canopy. Several men carried it using the large, wooden poles at the sides. They each had dark skin and black hair and wore longer tunics—and familiar-looking shoes.

The thief wore similar shoes.

I frowned, trying to recall exactly how tall he'd been. I looked from each man to the next, searching for any sign of recognition, but I was too far away to get a good look. I would need to get closer.

A nice springtime breeze blew softly, and the silk canopy shifted, revealing the solitary figure in the chair. The wind ruffled his small fan and the turban on his head, but he remained still.

"Nguyễn Văn Tường," I whispered, no doubt butchering the language. "The one who's supposed to meet with Philastre to sign the treaty."

As the litter made its way into the palace, I saw the French government officials and several military men preparing to greet Nguyễn.

Two maidservant women pulled the canopy back for their leader. Briefly, I saw their large, formal dresses of silk, with all their delicate designs of embroidery.

Hélène would have liked seeing them.

All of them had come together in their polite, stern circle, and then Nguyễn disembarked from his litter. I strode forward along with the rest of them; thanks to the Order and Lady Penelope, I was acting as Queen Victoria's selected representative. I pulled out the papers that gave me the official invitation, and the palace guards let me inside.

The palace itself was full of business and history, and I felt all the hallowed quality that came with age and prestige as I walked to the signing room.

Nguyễn and Philastre greeted each other in the signing room, and the service began.

Overall, it was relatively quiet. The next hour was spent going over the various details of the treaty. From what I could translate, that included the formal recognition of Annam as a kingdom, France's role in protecting it from its warring neighbors, and guaranteeing trade rights. There were

THE ORDER OF THE CRYSTAL DAGGERS

a few questions and replies, but then they signed their documents, and then it was time for the procession to leave.

I watched as all of this happened, and I was about to hail another carriage back to Hélène's quarters, satisfied with the calm turnout, when I saw him.

The thief from the day before was among those walking behind the Nguyễn's litter; I'd missed him on the way in, but as he passed me, his slanted eyes narrowed into angry slits, and he slowed in his pace, melting back into his native crowd.

I clenched my fists; I would have to find a way to capture him, and I would have to do it discretely. This was not the time to cause trouble, when representatives from two countries were watching.

I kept my eye firmly on the thief as I began to move forward. I walked briskly, not too fast, not too slow, but consistently; once the litter turned down the road toward the Port of Paris, I would make my move then.

The thief and I were of the same mind; the second the last carrier's shadow disappeared around the corner, we both took off.

"Not again," I grumbled under my breath.

Once more we raced through the streets. He was wearing the formal white robes of his country, so it was easy to spot him for a good while. By the time we reached the riverbanks, I saw he was trying to shed his outer robe gradually, letting himself fade into the rest of the crowds.

"Stop!" I called out.

It felt useless to say anything, and I felt even more discouraged when I passed by the same policeman from yesterday, and he began to call at me to stop, too.

"*Arrêtez!*"

Out the corner of my eye, I saw the thief stiffen; he recognized the policeman, too.

We raced ahead, just as the noontime church bells rang out through the city streets.

The bells must have given the thief an idea or two though, because he headed for the church entrance.

I was just thinking it was a shame Marguerite was not here when a horse neighed loudly.

Turning around, I was shocked to see Marguerite was riding atop the horse—and it was headed my way.

"Marguerite!" I scowled up at her. "What do you think you are doing?"

"Good morning to you, sir," Marguerite responded as I jumped aside to avoid getting run over. She wore her riding gown and bonnet with ease, and even from where I was, I could see her gloved hands had a firm, yet delicate grip on the reigns as she caught up to the thief.

He wasn't expecting her any more than I'd been.

She whirled the horse around in front of him. He tried to avoid it, but he ran right into the horse instead. As he strained to regain his balance, Marguerite jumped down from her sidesaddle.

As she landed squarely on top of him, I only wanted to grab her by the shoulders and scream at her for her recklessness.

Her horse was clearly uneasy by her sudden movement. It sidestepped, and the reins dragged along the ground.

I wanted to grab her by the shoulders and scream at her for her recklessness. Running up, I hauled Marguerite off the thief and both gently and angrily stood her on her feet.

"Marguerite," I growled. "Are you trying to give me a fit of apoplexy?"

THE ORDER OF THE CRYSTAL DAGGERS

"I was stopping him for you," Marguerite replied, fixing her bonnet, which had fallen askew when she'd jumped down. "And look, I got him—"

She was cut off as the thief jumped up, pushed himself between us, and shoved me down.

He grabbed Marguerite and held his arm around her throat dangerously.

She gasped in surprise as I scraped my leg on the cobblestone street.

"Marguerite!" I was screaming now with urgency as the thief held my wife hostage; no policeman was in sight, and people nearby scurried away as I feared the theif would strangle Marguerite. "Let her go—"

But Marguerite pulled out her fan; in the blink of an eye, she opened it up to reveal there were several long daggers hidden in the feathery folds. She stabbed him in the side.

He tightened his grip on her, but then he let her go as his side began to bleed significantly.

A moment later, he fell to the ground on his knees, and Marguerite knelt down next to him.

"Would you please stop?" I asked her. "You've done enough damage."

"I regret that I had to injure him," she said tightly. "But if you didn't want me to be here, you should've woken me up."

"You'd had a long night, and I didn't want you to worry about the treaty," I said. "You're here to see your sister. I figured you'd like the rest and you would appreciate the time with her."

"She's working this morning," Marguerite told me. "She's seeing to Prissy's training and getting her started with some basic rips and seams. She also has appointments with the ladies and courtesans of the city for measurements and fittings.”

“Well, I didn’t know that.” I rolled my eyes. “She didn’t mention that when I talked with her earlier.”

Marguerite frowned. “You spoke to her this morning?”

“Yes. She was having a cup of tea when I left.”

Marguerite scowled, and I didn’t really think that mattered too much, but at the groan from below us, I remembered the thief.

“Let’s take care of him, and then we can finish up this discussion later,” I said to Marguerite.

“I’m the better doctor.”

“I know, but I don’t want him to hurt you. And after what he tried to do to you, he doesn’t even deserve my help, little as it is.” I pressed down on the thief’s injury, trying to stop the bleeding. He squirmed and shouted at me angrily in his native tongue; after the signing, I knew he was from the Kingdom of Annam. “Do you know what he’s saying?” I asked Marguerite.

“Nothing kind,” she replied in a curt tone. “And I can’t blame him. You’re not going to stop the bleeding like that. In fact, I wouldn’t be surprised if—”

She broke off as the thief collapsed into unconsciousness.

Marguerite and I exchanged a glance with each other, and she shrugged. “Well, I was about to say I wouldn’t be surprised if he fainted.”

“He’s been quite the headache for us, but at least he’s getting it as much as he’d giving it,” I said.

“Ben, that is not kind.”

THE ORDER OF THE CRYSTAL DAGGERS

I wanted to remind her that she was the one who'd nearly run him down with a horse, but I only shrugged. "What do you suggest?"

"Let's take him back to Hélène's." Marguerite skipped over to where the horse she'd been riding had gone. It was only a little way from us.

I looked back at her horse, which seemed docile enough. "Where did you get the horse?"

"I borrowed him from Hélène's neighbor, once I realized I was late to the signing," she said.

"He let you borrow it?"

"That's what I said, *mon amour.*" Marguerite gave me a cool smile. "I thought it would be rather unexpected. Don't you agree?"

I decided not say anything. I did wonder if Hélène's neighbor knew that she'd borrowed the horse or not, but either way, I was actually secretly pleased she did. That meant I wouldn't be forced to carry the bleeding thief on my own.

We loaded the thief up onto the saddle carefully, and then each of us took a side as we headed back toward Hélène's shop.

"We'll go around the back," Marguerite said as we headed down a block further than we needed. "That way I can return the horse while you get him up to bed."

I didn't think the thief needed the comfort of a bed, but I didn't say anything to Marguerite. She would only object, saying he needed care, and we would have to tend to him if we wanted to learn why he stole the painting, and she probably did feel bad about hurting him, even if he'd tried to hurt her first.

"Do you think it's a good idea to take him back to Hélène's when we still have the painting there?" I asked Marguerite.

THE ORDER OF THE CRYSTAL DAGGERS

"What choice do we have, Ben?" She looked back at the unconscious man on the horse. "We can't leave him. His wound needs treated."

His wound that you caused, I wanted to say, but I refrained.

"Now that the signing is over, I'll go and take the painting to the Louvre," I said. "That way, we won't be risking the painting's theft a second time."

"And what should I do?" Marguerite asked.

"You stay and watch over him," I grumbled, barely hiding my frustration. It looked like Marguerite had managed to find a way to work with me on my mission after all. "I'll tie him down before I leave, so you'll be safe if he wakes up while I'm gone."

Marguerite gave me a dazzling smile. "Sounds good, *mon amour*."

"Yes," I said. "It sounds good—to you, at least."

7

◊

I was worried that the thief would wake up again before I left. It had been easy for him to escape me the first time he'd passed out, and I was not angling for a repeat experience.

This time, it appeared he was in much worse condition; after Marguerite and I had him tied down firmly to a spare bed, he still hadn't woken up.

So, I packed up the painting he'd been carrying and I headed out, once more hailing a carriage as I headed to the Louvre. I wasn't happy about leaving Marguerite, but I did want to clear my name and make sure the painting was secured. And it was nice to get a bit more of a rest in after chasing the thief from the Luxembourg Palace to Notre Dame. It had been several blocks, and I hadn't fully recovered from the previous day's run.

The Louvre had been one of France's finest palaces before it had been transformed into a museum. Several hallways and adjoining buildings were part of the palace but not part of the public display, and a number of construction projects had been underway for decades now, in efforts to take surrounding buildings and join them in with the Louvre. While there were various historical reasons for the project, and I could see it was all very grand; I was glad that I was able to find the service entrance without much difficulty.

After the chase yesterday, and then this morning, it unnerved me that so many policemen lined the hallways, but at least none of them looked familiar. Still, I kept an eye on them as I walked to meet with the curator, a man named Phillippe de Marsden.

He was a bright, energetic-looking man, with a flop of gray-speckled brown hair and a matching mustache that was neatly trimmed. He was wearing a suit that was professional, but it was covered with grime and paint at various spots. I didn't mind; he greeted me with warmth, and then suspicion, as I explained to him the unique situation.

"Well," he said eagerly, "I can see why they let you in, if it's truly Delacroix's Marianne. I have heard some concerns about your person, but since you mean to give me the painting, and you're not asking for money, I am willing to inspect your claims."

"Thank you," I said. I didn't like that my integrity was questioned, but it wasn't as if the man knew me, or even knew of me.

With the help of de Marsden and his assistants, I pulled out the painting carefully. He glanced it over and pulled out a large glass, examining different portions of the canvas.

"How did you come to own this?" he asked, frowning as he moved. His earlier excitement was gone, and his eyes were full of concern.

"I stole it from a thief," I admitted.

"A thief?"

"I figure it's not wrong to steal something that's been stolen, as long as it goes back to its rightful owner."

"Is that so?" de Marsden's scowl deepened. "I've been told the rumors about a thief with a crippled leg, who was stealing this from a rather popular Salon."

"I'm not the thief," I scoffed. "Or at least, not the original one. I just told you so."

"Yes, you did admit you stole it," de Marsden said angrily. "And I suspect, with that kind of caviler attitude, I have very little hope you're not here to try to claim some reward after all."

THE ORDER OF THE CRYSTAL DAGGERS

"What do you mean?" I asked. "This is the painting I found, and I told you I'm here to return it."

"Do you think I'm a fool? I am the curator here at the Louvre, the most acclaimed museum and collection of art in the modern world!" Phillippe looked indignant as he shook his head and gestured toward one of the guards at the door. "And this is a forgery."

"A fake?" I repeated. "But—"

"It's a very good one, sir, and one of the better ones, for certain," he continued, as the guard came up behind me. "But this is not Delacroix's true work."

"Why would I lie to you?" I asked, pushing back.

"Well, if you have nothing to hide, you wouldn't run away, for one," Phillippe said. "And another, I suspect this is a forgery that you intended to turn over to us, and, when you and your thieving cohorts went to sell the original, we would assume this one is the real one. But you underestimate us, sir."

"I didn't know it was a fake," I insisted, ducking as another guard tried to catch me.

"You're a very good actor, but just like this painting, it's all falsehoods and lies in the end." Phillippe shook his head. "For shame, too. Have you no decency, sir?"

It was more than ironic, I thought. I was trying to return a painting that had been presumed lost, only to find out it was a forgery, and then get accused of working with the original thief.

"There were rumors of art thieves decades ago," Phillippe continued. "They were ambitious, wanting to secure and replace the world's most treasured pieces with their own fakes. France has always been the envy of the world; but it is precisely because of that, I have made a most meticulous study, and I will not be misled."

"This was just a mistake," I reiterated, but it was to no avail. Phillippe wouldn't listen to me.

"Didn't you hear me?" Phillippe scoffed. "I will not be made a fool over this. Guards, arrest him, and then escort my assistants to the junk pile. This forgery needs to be burned with the rest of our discards at the end of the day."

Phillippe would not listen; I had no choice but to run for it.

As I made my escape, I sincerely hoped our thief would be awake by the time I got back to Marguerite and her sister. I needed some answers, and it was clear he was the only one who could give them to me.

THE ORDER OF THE CRYSTAL DAGGERS

8

◊

"Marguerite, come quickly." I stepped into Hélène's house, eager to find a place to sit down and rest.

Not without some difficulty, I had escaped the Louvre, and made the long way back to Hélène's shop. The run home had been long and spread out, and while I'd been able to take more breaks than when I had been chasing after the thief, I was still exhausted, and I wanted nothing more than to rest my feet.

I didn't hear a response, so I headed toward the parlor, wondering if perhaps she was talking with Hélène or even Prissy some.

I was surprised to see all of them sitting there, nervously looking at each other in silence.

"Hello, ladies," I said, suddenly realizing something was dreadfully wrong. "What is—?"

At the small, familiar *click* of a bullet entering the shaft chamber, I froze and went silent, too.

I glanced to the side, expecting to see the thief we'd caught earlier.

But to my surprise, it wasn't him.

It was a woman—the same woman Marguerite had tried to help the previous day.

"I see you found Madame Phénix's shop," I said dryly.

"Be quiet," the woman muttered in English. "I have come here for my brother—and our painting. I want them now."

"Your painting?" I needed to keep her talking, distracting her as my fingers slid down to the dagger at my side. "You mean the fake painting? The forgery of Delacroix's *Liberty Leading the People*?"

She went quiet for a long moment, before I realized she was trying to translate my words in her head. I thought about repeating myself, but she eventually nodded.

"Yes. It is our painting." She held the gun up more firmly to my temple. "I demand you give it to me along with my brother."

"Who are you?" I asked, stepping back.

"You don't know?" she huffed. "I should not be surprised to see that the family of Louis Valoris does not recognize me. They do not acknowledge their victims."

"What?" My jaw tightened. "We're not part of the Valoris family. Why would you think that? We're nothing like that lying, murderous—"

I was about to tell her she had her information wrong, and that she was mistaken—and unlike Phillippe de Marsden, I would be willing to hear her side of the story.

But just at that moment, Marguerite let out a frightened moan, and I turned to look at her.

And this time, I *really* looked at her.

For all the years of our marriage, I'd never before noticed how some of her features—even the more prominent ones, like her crystalline green eyes or her blond curls—suddenly reminded me of Lumiere.

Before, I'd never noticed it; and now, it was uncanny.

My jaw went slack as the truth struck me hard, and my heart sank.

All other thoughts—the foreign woman, her injured brother, the painting, the gun—fled.

How could my sweet, beloved Marguerite be related to the insidious Louis Valoris—the same Louis Valoris who was a murderer, the mastermind behind the world's end, and the one who'd damaged and destroyed so much of my family?

"I told you to tell him the truth," Hélène whispered.

I turned to glare over at her, wanting to rebuke her for doubting me; but then I saw the similarity in her distinctive eyebrows and her pouted lips, and it struck me hard that I'd married into Louis and Lumiere's family.

"How?" I finally asked.

"Louis was our father," Marguerite whispered quietly, as her eyes fill with tears. "We are his illegitimate offspring. We didn't know until our mother died. She must have suspected he might come after her at some point, because she named him in her will."

"We think he had her killed," Hélène added. "Although there is no way to prove it now. But our mother was a shrewd, ruthless woman of business herself, and she knew too much about his ambitions."

"What of Lumiere?" I asked. "Does he know?"

"He is our half-brother. He doesn't know. Or at least, we don't think so," Marguerite admitted, glancing over at Hélène, who nodded in agreement. "We only truly know the power and reputation behind Louis Valoris' name, which is why we vowed never to speak of it."

"What about Lady Penelope?" I asked, suddenly curious. It did seem very strange my grandmother, Louis' long-time rival and archenemy, would be the very person to save his illegitimate daughters from a life of professional prostitution and never mention it to me. "Does she know?"

"No." Marguerite shook her head. "Neither of us ever mentioned it to her."

THE ORDER OF THE CRYSTAL DAGGERS

I didn't know what to think of that; I was more willing to bet Lady Penelope *did* know.

All of my earlier desire to learn of the painting and its origins had been summarily dismissed inside my mind; I was flustered and unexpectedly caught off guard by the revelation.

But the woman pressed the barrel of her gun into my temple again, once more demanding our attention.

"I want my brother, and our painting," she insisted. She seemed to realize I was stunned by the revelation of Marguerite's lineage, and that she had missed something after all. "I waited for you to return; I will not wait any longer now that you can see I will kill you and your family if you do not give me what I want."

"Your brother, or the man I assume to be your brother, is upstairs resting," I said. "I ran into him earlier. He did not escape unscathed."

She paused again, and I clarified, "He's hurt."

"What happened?" she asked. "Did you hurt him?"

"Yes, but I did not mean to." I heard Marguerite whimper again; she knew I was protecting her from the woman's anger. "My wife has been caring for him."

The woman looked crushed, and her aim faltered as her shoulders slumped forward in despair.

"Please," Marguerite said as she stood up.

The woman jerked back up her gun in Marguerite's direction, and I couldn't risk it; I whipped out my dagger, letting the blade of the *Wahabite Jambiya* strike; the gun fell out of the woman's grasp, and I hurried to kick it away from her.

The woman screamed in frustration as Hélène grabbed the fallen gun, and Marguerite pulled her toward the small couch. I sat down on her one side and gripped her arm, while

Marguerite sat down on the other side; much as we had earlier with the thief on the horse, we secured her between us.

"Hélène," I said. "Go and see if her brother is awake."

"Prissy is tending to him," Marguerite told me. "I had her stay upstairs when Hélène called me."

Hélène nodded toward the woman. "She told me she was an ambassador for Nguyễn Văn Tường. She wanted me to see about creating a style for the Kingdom of Annam, making dresses and *ao dai*, their traditional formal wear."

"I saw your brother with Nguyễn earlier," I said, surprising the woman. "He was one of his servants."

The woman nodded. "Yes. We both work for Nguyễn. It was the only way we could come to Paris."

"Why did you want to come here?" Marguerite looked at her curiously. "Was it because of Louis Valoris?"

The woman glared at her and went silent.

"I am sorry," Marguerite said, her eyes on the ground. "But I vow, my sister and I are not like our father. We do not support him or anything that he has done. We do not even know what he did in many instances."

"You are lying."

"No, we're not," Marguerite insisted. "We will prove it to you. We will let you go, and we will give you your brother, and your painting, too."

I cleared my throat. "Well, actually—"

Before I could tell them what happened to the painting, Hélène came down the stairs with the thief behind her. Prissy was behind him, helping him stay upright. I noticed his nose had a small scratch on it, and there was a large bandage wrapped around his torso.

I didn't need to ask; I could guess that Marguerite and Prissy had patched him up after my lackluster job earlier.

When the thief saw his sister, he immediately brightened up. "Thuy!"

We all exchanged looks, but the woman jumped up from between me and Marguerite, and she went running up to him.

"Tho," she exclaimed happily. "I am so happy you are alive. I thought they would kill you."

"They helped me with my wounds," Tho replied. He glared over at me. "But they also caused them."

"I was only trying to stop you from getting away with thievery," I explained.

"Ben, say you're sorry," Prissy insisted. "He's a nice young man and he's injured, too."

"Yes, Mr. Ben," Tho said. "Say you're sorry."

If I had been less shocked by Marguerite's secret, I might have been amused by the entire situation. Thuy's determination for justice was understandable, Tho's battered state could have been avoided, but I was baffled by Prissy's assertiveness. It seemed my stepsister had been charmed by her patient, and at a most inconvenient time.

Tho and Thuy turned to look at me.

Now that I saw them together, I realized they were likely twins; they were around the same age, height, and learning, and they even seemed more coordinated in their movements and mannerisms than most individuals.

If I knew anything about siblings on mission, they were to be taken seriously.

"I'm Benedict Svoboda," I said, giving them a formal introduction. "I am a member of the Order of the Crystal Daggers, and I came here to oversee the signing of the

Philastre Treaty. This is my wife, Marguerite, and her sister, Hélène."

"Madame Phénix," Thuy murmured, and I nodded.

"This is also my stepsister, Priscilla," I said, gesturing toward her.

"We've met," Tho replied, making me scowl as Prissy smiled.

"I am Khang Von Thuy, and this is my brother, Khang Von Tho," Thuy said. "Now, where is our painting?"

"I took it to the Louvre," I said. "It is an art museum. The curator is the one who told me it is a fake."

Tho and Thuy did not look surprised in the least.

"We know," Tho said. "Our mother was the one who painted it."

I looked back to Marguerite and Hélène, and I started to realize how everything was connected. I thought back to what Ella had told me about our mother's last mission to Prague, about Louis' devious plans involving an art ring, and even Phillippe de Marsden's earlier tale of forgeries.

"Your mother was one of Louis Valoris' artists," I said. "He used a lot of them to make forgeries of famous works throughout Europe and the known world."

Thuy and Tho nodded in unison.

"The Order worked against him," I said quietly. "My own mother worked on such a case."

"Our mother was a great talent," Thuy said. "Louis Valoris brought the original of our painting to her in Saigon, and she painted it. It was a perfect match."

"Some of the paint compositions must have been different, and perhaps the canvas material, too," I said, thinking of how

THE ORDER OF THE CRYSTAL DAGGERS

de Marsden had examined the painting. "But if it was in its frame, no one would be able to tell."

"Yes." Tho nodded. "She died many years ago; we suspect one of her rivals killed her, or even because of Louis Valoris himself. We have been struggling to find all her paintings. The one I stole earlier was her first forgery. There are several others around Europe that are hers, too."

I glanced over at Marguerite. If what they were saying was true—and it seemed like it was—then it was certainly something the Order should investigate.

She nodded in agreement, but then she looked down in shame.

"We want her work back," Thuy continued. "They are the only things we have left of her now. It is hard for others to understand our desires, but we want them to remind us of her."

"My mother died a long time ago, too." I heard myself say the words before I realized I was speaking. Quickly, I brushed aside my embarrassment and stepped forward. "I understand you more than you can ever know."

I thought back to the book Marguerite had found for me just the day before; I thought of how happy Ella would be to know we'd found it. Holding it had been holding onto a piece of my past, and a piece of our family history.

Yes, I understood Tho and Thuy very well in that moment. I could even understand their hatred of Louis Valoris, knowing how he'd tormented Lady Penelope and my mother over the years before his suicide.

Long silence passed between us, and then Thuy reached out her hand.

"We would like our painting now."

THE ORDER OF THE CRYSTAL DAGGERS

I cringed. "I told you, I don't have it. I would give it to you, but I left it at the Louvre when they accused me of working with a gang of art thieves."

Tho and Thuy both frowned.

"You do not have it?" Tho asked again, as if he had not understood me.

I shook my head. "No. But I will do everything I can to help you get it back. If you will come with me now, we will get it back before the day is over."

And we will have to. Otherwise, their painting will burn.

"What do you want us to do?" Tho asked. He inhaled sharply. "I may not be much good."

"I will hire a carriage," Hélène said before she rushed from the room.

"I will help with Tho's injuries," Prissy volunteered.

"And I will follow your directions," Marguerite promised.

Her comment made me pause; I could tell from her expression she was still unsure of how shocked I was, and she didn't want to cross me. I wanted to talk to her, to ask questions, and try to figure things out.

But there were more pressing matters to attend to. If my mother's book was about to get burned, as Tho and Thuy's mother's painting was, I would not want anything to stop me. As we all lined up to load into a carriage, I pulled her aside.

"We will talk later," I said. "For now, stay where I can see you."

"I wouldn't let you down," Marguerite insisted. "And I wouldn't betray you."

I put my hands on her shoulders. "We will talk later," I reiterated. "We have a job to do."

"We?"

I was at least a little gratified to see she was not certain how to take the news that she would be joining me on our outing, even if I still worried for her safety.

Grimly, I nodded. "Yes."

THE ORDER OF THE CRYSTAL DAGGERS

9

◊

Even before we arrived at the Louvre, I knew getting inside would be much harder, especially since I'd run away earlier, and there were still guards around. Whether they recognized me or not, I was certain that it wasn't common for a "crippled thief" to bring in a painting, expect no compensation, and then fight to take his leave.

"Listen," I said. "The Louvre is a big palace. I'm not sure where they took your painting. We'll have to make a plan."

"Why can we not run in?" Tho asked.

"They think your painting was from a criminal art forgery ring," I tried to explain. "They will think you're the villain."

Just as I did, until about an hour ago.

I did not say that part aloud.

I glanced over at Marguerite, who was huddled in the seat next to me, still unwilling to meet my gaze. She was the one who taught me I could never expect the unexpected. I was starting to realize that in expecting the unexpected anyway, the unexpected only became more absurd.

Here I was, teaming up with twins, helping them recover their mother's painting, which was linked all the way back to Louis Valoris and my own mother's memory, too.

"Here's what we're going to do," I said. "Tho, you're injured, so you're going to walk toward the servant's entrance in the back, the one where I went in earlier. Prissy, you walk with him."

"That's fine with me," Prissy agreed, tightening her arm around Tho's.

"You're going to walk until you're about halfway between the street and the door," I said to Tho. "Then, I want you to pretend that you're sick and you need help. You need to faint. I know you can manage that."

Tho made a face at me, but he nodded.

"Then, Prissy, you start crying and get them to come and help you pick Tho up."

"Yes," Prissy agreed. "I can do that."

"Are you sure?" I'd never seen her cry before, but I wasn't about to assign Marguerite the role instead.

She squared her shoulders with pride. "Yes. I'm good at looking helpless."

I wasn't going to argue with her.

"Thuy," I said, turning to her. "You're going to go to the front. You'll pretend to be the ambassador for Nguyễn Văn Tường again. I know you can do that well."

"So do I," Hélène agreed with a begrudging smile.

I ignored her, as I pointed to Thuy's gun, the one she'd tried to use on us earlier. "Once you're inside, you—"

"What do I do? Do I shoot someone?" Thuy asked.

She reminded me of Ella so much in that moment, and while I knew my sister was a weakness, it was such a weakness that gave me the strength to fight harder. It was understood between us that we were no longer enemies, but allies. As I met Thuy's gaze, I had the feeling it was possible we might even be friends one day, if our mission went well.

"Hopefully not." I almost smiled. "Pretend that you're here for your scheduled tour, and that Nguyễn Văn Tường has personally requested Phillippe de Marsden, the curator, as your guide. Hélène, you go with her as her translator. See if you can find out where the burning pile is located. I heard

Phillippe de Marsden say he wanted to burn your mother's painting, since it was such an excellent forgery."

After another long moment, Thuy nodded, and then I looked to Marguerite.

"You and I will sneak in after the others provide the distraction," I said. "Go follow Prissy and Tho, and sneak in the back."

"What should we do after the guards come?" Prissy asked.

"Have them take you and Tho to a room inside the Louvre," I said. "That way, they can provide him with medical treatment. If they won't do that, have them escort you to a carriage again, and go home. We will meet you later. There's nothing else the rest of us will be able to help you."

"You seem to have all of this planned out," Hélène said, amused. "It seems that you've inherited Lady Penelope's famed intellect."

"Well, Ella got my mother's looks; I had to get something from the family, too," I replied, watching as Marguerite smiled. I could almost see her thoughts; we both knew if I'd waited to return the painting, none of our planning would be necessary. "Now, does anyone have any questions?"

A moment passed in silence before my wife spoke up.

"If we find the painting, how do we get out?" Marguerite asked.

"As fast as you can." I tried to give her a smile, but it was impossible to smile when she seemed so miserable.

Instead, I took a deep breath and shifted my focus.

I would talk with her later. I had more pressing concerns at the moment. Once I solved the problem I'd helped cause, I could move on to the next bit of trouble without worry.

THE ORDER OF THE CRYSTAL DAGGERS

◊　　◊　　◊　　◊

The plan seemed simple enough, but it wasn't flawless. I'd taken everyone's strengths and weaknesses into consideration, and I'd given them the push to do what they did best.

I'd planned it all out, and now I had to hope for the best, and then leave it at that.

Hélène and Thuy alighted down from the carriage first, since we were passing by the main entrance. I decided to wait until everyone else had gone to their assigned locations to loop around and follow after Hélène and Thuy. I watched as they went down and headed off, and I had to fight the urge not to yell out further instructions before the carriage rolled on.

When Prissy and Tho left next, it was just me and Marguerite left.

I looked at her, but she still did not want to look at me.

Is she worried I'll only think of Lumiere when I see her? Or maybe I'd think of how much I hate Louis for all his cruelty?

I couldn't imagine what was going on inside her mind. I would just have to wait and talk with her later.

"Marguerite." I took her hands in mine, but she jerked away from me. I sighed and let her go, as it was time for us to move, too. "Please be safe."

"I will." She finally gave me a small glimpse, before she nodded.

"Once we get the painting, we can leave and go home," I said.

She only winced, and I didn't know what else to say.

I got down from our carriage, paid the driver, and then we also sped off.

THE ORDER OF THE CRYSTAL DAGGERS

Already, I could hear Prissy wailing at the top of her lungs, as Tho twitched on the ground, grabbing his side and crying out in pain. It looked like they were both eager for careers on the stage, should the occasion call for it.

I almost said this to Marguerite, but she was already gone, slipping inside the servant door I'd walked through earlier, as the guards tried to pacify both Prissy and Tho.

I disappeared down an alleyway, looking for a way inside. I tripped and fell by accident as my bad leg caught on a garbage bin lid. It was then I thought of Ferdy and his clever use of disguises, and I rubbed more grime on my clothes, and walked out, exaggerating my limp.

"Help," I whimpered, engaging in my own acting abilities with a sense of personal humiliation. "I've been robbed."

Some of the guards came to see me, and it wasn't long before I'd managed to talk my way inside the Louvre—and once I was inside, I followed up my act using my sister's favorite trick.

"I need to excuse myself," I said. "I fear I need to use the washroom."

No one bothered to question me.

I made my way through the large palace, looking for different rooms, wondering where the painting could have gone. It was a very large, grueling job, and my leg ached again with overuse; I would need to rest, and really rest, before I did any strenuous exercise.

It was only when I heard Phillippe de Marsden's voice again that I cheered up. I could hear him talking to Hélène while Thuy was speaking in her native language fervently. Beside her, Hélène gave her best charming act to Phillippe, who looked absolutely dazzled by her attentions, as she pretended to translate Thuy's words.

THE ORDER OF THE CRYSTAL DAGGERS

"My client heard that you had some of Delacroix's work here," Hélène said. "She is most interested in his Lady Liberty."

"That's so strange," Phillippe said, but he brightened up as Hélène let him take her arm and escort her more closely. "I specifically had a fake version of that painting taken out back to the gardens. As it is a fake, it's not right to let it remain; others would get confused. In fact, I'm certain that you must have heard that from one of the worker boys here; they're ignorant and they know nothing of true art, let alone how to identify a forgery."

"So it is a forgery?" Hélène pressed. "How do you know?"

"Why, I examined it myself, and while the painting was excellent, and the quality was high, the canvas was made of rice leaves," he explained. "Papyrus was the main paper of the Egyptians, and the Far East has rice plants. You can tell a culture by its paper, you know."

"Oh, do go on," Hélène said, as Thuy went quiet. She had a look of pride on her face as they continued to walk down the hall.

"Good," I muttered under my breath. "The painting is in the back gardens."

Quietly as possible, I signaled Thuy. She saw me at once, and gave me an almost imperceivable nod.

Even without knowing her long, I knew she had gotten my message. She was doing a good job at distracting the curator, and we knew where to look—and that was where I was headed.

As I made my way there, I overheard servants complaining about "the spoiled little rich girl" and her "foreign husband" who was clearly hoping to die thanks to how tightly she clung to him.

I grinned; Prissy was playing her part well, too.

I was just wondering where Marguerite was when we both stepped into the back gardens; she came from the east side, and I came from the west.

Her face lit up briefly. "Ben."

I gave her a slight bow. "Madame."

"You heard that the painting was here, too, did you?"

I nodded. "Let's find it and get out of here, shall we?"

She smiled. "I think I've seen enough art today."

Together, it didn't take the two of us long to find the painting. It had been thrown in a pile of other items; dirty curtains, stained, incomplete canvasses, and even some damaged frames.

It was strange to see such damaged beauty in a garden that was full of lovely plants and just-blooming bushes and flowers.

Without a word, Marguerite and I pulled the fake painting from the pile, smoothed it out, and folded it carefully. She then handed it to me.

"Thank you," I said, as we turned back to leave.

"Did I listen to you?" Marguerite asked, her voice full of hesitation. "Are you pleased?"

"I think everyone did a good job so far," I said. "See if you can let them know we got it, and they can leave now. I'll sneak out and get a carriage. And then we can go home."

"I will do that," Marguerite said. Her voice was still gloomy, and I knew she was still unsure of how I felt.

I wasn't entirely sure of that myself, but I was certain that Louis Valoris would never bother to steal a fake painting from a secure museum, nor would he make friends with the people he'd chased all over the city the day before.

And knowing that, it gave me hope.

THE ORDER OF THE CRYSTAL DAGGERS

10

◊

Not for the first time, it was pure relief to get back to Hélène's shop.

Tho and Thuy were very pleased to have their mother's painting back; Hélène and Prissy were lively, excited to have been helpful in a real spy mission. Marguerite was the only one who seemed distant, but even she answered questions and told the others about how she'd listened to my instructions perfectly.

Everyone else seemed eager to exchange stories and hear what had happened in the museum. While I was just happy no one had been caught, arrested, or killed, all the running around and the stress had worn me out.

I was nodding off as the carriage rolled up to the shop.

"I know we said we would talk later," I said to Marguerite. "But it has been a very long day, and I am tired. We can talk in the morning, if that suits you."

She paused for a moment, and then nodded. "If that is your wish."

I arched my brow at her again. "I thought you said I wouldn't want a wife who would follow me blindly."

"My faith in you is not blind," Marguerite said quietly, though there was a depressed quality to her expression. "I do want to say something first. I want you to know that I'm aware I broke the trust between us by not telling you the truth about my father. I do hope you'll be able to forgive me for that. But I still love you and I want to remain your wife, even though I know your family hates mine."

"Marguerite, don't—"

I reached for her, but she shook her head. She stepped back, gave me a quick curtsy, and then excused herself.

"I'll see you in the morning," she murmured, before she left.

Before I could follow her, I felt a tug on my other sleeve.

I turned to see Tho there. He was still holding his side a little uneasily, but he was smiling.

"Mr. Ben," he said. "My sister and I have been talking, and we would like to work with you."

"Work with me?" I repeated, as though I wasn't sure I'd heard him correctly.

"Yes. You know a lot about this spy business. And we can help the Order you were talking about, too. We have some of our mother's notes about her paintings. If we work together, we might be able to find more."

"Yes," Thuy agreed. "And you could teach us more. We do not know how to do spy work like you do. Would the Order accept orphans such as us?"

I looked at Thuy's young face, and Tho's eager expression.

I thought back to my own early days working with Lady Penelope, and Amir, and Harshad, and how I'd longed for a place to belong and a purpose to serve.

I knew what it was like to be in their position. They were orphaned, alone except each other, determined to honor their mother's legacy.

Who could teach them better than me?

"Well … " I glanced back toward the door Marguerite had disappeared through. She'd told me before that Lady Penelope would like to see me progress in the Order, and pass on what I'd learned.

THE ORDER OF THE CRYSTAL DAGGERS

It looked like I would be able to not only be a mentor, but I would be able to find my own students, too—starting with two of them.

In some ways, I could almost see Ella's smile twinkling through Thuy's bright brown eyes. And it wasn't hard for me to remember my own resolve to succeed when I'd first started; looking at Tho, it was clear he had that same determination, too.

"I would be honored to teach you," I finally said.

They both bowed to me, and then they both reached out and took hold of my hands.

Thuy smiled reverently. "Thank you, Teacher."

Tho glanced up. "We welcome your instruction. We promise to do well, in honor of our mother."

I gripped their hands back tightly in my own, truly touched by the gift of their time and their trust.

I had a feeling the next few weeks would be hard on them, and maybe on me, too.

All of us would be squashed into Hélène's quarters—but we could make ourselves a home here.

Yes. Everything will be fine. We can make it work. I can just think of it as another new mission.

I looked up at Thuy and Tho. "You're welcome. We'll start training tomorrow afternoon. Before we begin, I have to draw up some plans, and I should write a letter to Lady Penelope, to let her know we will be staying in Paris a little while longer." I glanced behind me again, looking for Marguerite, even though I knew she'd gone up to bed. "And there's something important that I need to take care of tomorrow morning, too."

11

◊

I fell asleep fast, but the next morning, when I woke up, I found I'd been dreaming of *Otec* and *Máma*, of Ella and Ferdy; I thought about Lady POW and Harshad, of Hélène and Prissy, and Marguerite, too, and I thought about how my family had done a fair job of growing in the last few years.

In the distance, I could hear the sound of the Cathedral's church bells.

Was it really Sunday already?

I opened my eyes to see my wife sleeping peacefully on the bed, curled away from me. Her hair was a tangled mess of curls as she breathed in deeply and peacefully. I pushed a curl back from her forehead, watching her in wonder. Watching her was magic, and hearing the call of the day's beginning felt like the spell was breaking—but it was only breaking into something more beautiful.

I reached over, pulling Marguerite against me.

"What is it?" she murmured sleepily.

"Get up and get dressed," I whispered. "And hurry. We have to get going."

"Do we have a mission today?"

"Yes," I said. "We do."

Marguerite finally opened her eyes; she was more than a little confused, but she still did as I requested.

Quietly, the two of us made our way through Hélène's house and sneaked out the back door; I was in a good mood, and enough so that even my leg didn't seem quite so painful this morning.

We began to walk, and Marguerite asked me all sorts of questions before she gave up.

I kept my silence; I wouldn't tell her where we were going.

It was only when the Notre Dame Cathedral came into view, and we began to walk up to its majestic entrance that Marguerite fell completely silent. I held onto her hand, which was trembling, and I was surprised to see her eyes filling with tears as we entered into the sacred building.

"What is it?" I lowered my voice. "Did I do something wrong?"

"No. It's just … I have been wanting to come here with you," Marguerite whispered. "More than anything. With everything that happened since we've come, I almost forgot."

"It's no matter. I remembered." I tightened her hand in mine as we entered into the sanctuary of the Notre Dame Cathedral. Its grand buttresses, the high vaulted ceilings, and the delicately ornate altar immersed us in an otherworldly setting. There were people in the pews, preparing for the morning mass, and several of the church's priests and attendants were scurrying around as they prepared for service.

"After my mother died, I used to come here when I couldn't sleep," Marguerite confessed.

"Back when you and Hélène were still running your mother's … business?"

She nodded, even as she shivered. A brothel was a sordid business, even if it was still a "business."

"I used to cry and pray to be rescued from my troubles. I used to dream that despite the obstacles I had from my birth and background, I would be able to find a husband who could love me."

"Of course, you would." I could hardly believe that it was a point of pain for her to believe herself unlovable, especially

THE ORDER OF THE CRYSTAL DAGGERS

since I, as her husband, got to love her as no one else would. "Who could resist loving you?"

"Are you certain you should ask me that?" Marguerite asked. "I know of plenty who can resist; some of the people Hélène and I blackmailed wanted us dead. Men don't actually want to marry prostitutes. And of course, my own father, whether I knew him or not, was a monster and a murderer."

"You are not who he is, Marguerite," I told her. "That's why I brought you here."

She looked around. "What?"

"I wanted to tell you, on hallowed, sacred ground, that I still love you, and I still want you to be my wife," I said. "It's true our families have complicated histories; but why should that stop us from finding love, especially among all the hate? That is what love does, after all."

Marguerite finally smiled at me—that smile I loved, the one bursting with sunlight and joy.

"You know, when Hélène was all finished setting her new identity and her shop, I left Paris with Lady Penelope. I'd never felt so free in all my life. But I did feel bad. I had to stop coming here, to this place, to wish away my shame, even if I still carried it, and soon enough, I forgot my dreams."

She looked all around, taking in the brilliantly lit windows, full of light and sunshine. I could almost see her memories, as she remembered how desperate she'd felt as she lit a candle by the altar, praying for a future she found unattainable.

"You can't understand how wonderful I feel, standing here beside you, Ben." When she turned back to face me, her eyes were shining with happy tears. "You are a miracle—a miracle to me, and a miracle for me. Even when we were first together, you didn't have to marry me; I would have taken any position to be with you—lover, mistress, nurse, student. Anything at all."

THE ORDER OF THE CRYSTAL DAGGERS

I took both her hands in mine. "It's not just your prayer that has been answered; I don't think I ever even dared to voice mine. I am glad I have you as my wife."

Discreetly as possible, I leaned over. The whole room lit, blazing with the colors of the rose window, as I kissed her softly on the lips.

I closed my eyes at the taste of her, and my vision swirled with light and color, falling into love's messy, warm, and radiant embrace. My heart felt as dazzling and deep as any impressionist work of art, and Marguerite was twice as captivating—and in that moment, I knew that I would only be drawn more in as the years passed and we faced down all our days together.

"I love you," I whispered.

"I love you, too." Marguerite pulled away and smiled up at me, bright enough to rival the sun itself. "And no one will ever be able to stop me from doing so."

"That's just as well, since I don't intend to let you stop." I leaned in to kiss her.

"Wait," Marguerite said, putting her finger over my lips. "Does this mean you'll let me come on more missions with you now? Now you know I have a stellar spy pedigree, in addition to Lady Penelope's training."

She was teasing me, but just like Ella, Marguerite was a weakness in my heart that compelled me to become stronger.

"I think I will have to bring you along now," I said. "We can't have someone like you left to her own devices for too long without supervision. But you must promise me two things."

"Yes. Anything."

"We have no more secrets between us," I said.

"That's fair."

"And you'll follow my directions."

"As long as you answer all my questions, I will agree to that." Marguerite's mischievousness lit up her emerald eyes as the morning sunshine blazed through the rose-stained glass and baptized us in a sea of color and light.

"We'll work it out," I said, unable to stop myself from leaning in.

The church bells began to ring again, and their music was a resounding, heavenly harkening, only perfected all the more by Marguerite's muted laughter as I kissed her.

THE ORDER OF THE CRYSTAL DAGGERS

C. S. Johnson is an award-winning, genre-hopping author of several novels, including *The Starlight Chronicles* series, the *Once Upon a Princess* saga, and the *Divine Space Pirates* trilogy. With a gift for sarcasm and an apologetic heart, she currently lives in Atlanta with her family.

THE ORDER OF THE CRYSTAL DAGGERS

AUTHOR'S NOTE

Dear Reader,

I hope you don't mind my indulgence in this matter. Leaving The Order of the Crystal Daggers behind was difficult for me, and I am not really that surprised to find myself writing this companion novella—especially since I started writing it before *Heart of Hope and Fear* was even finished.

There were a few things that went into this one with the rawness of an open wound.

A few years ago, in 2019, I watched in horror as Notre Dame Cathedral began to burn. Eventually the spire collapsed and the roof, centuries old and its secrets well-guarded, collapsed. I am truly grateful for the French fire department workers who sought to save it, including the relics, but as I watched it burn I felt as though a part of my own heart was on fire. I wept at the loss, and later, I wept out of gratefulness for what was saved. I couldn't stop the pain or the change, but I am grateful for what is left, and what can be sustained.

At the heart of this novel, I think that this is what Ben also realizes.

There is good in tearing down tyranny, if it is all tyranny; but something better still must be built up in its place. While Ben's pain at the loss of his mother, father, and Amir is still there, he realizes without those losses, he never would have met Marguerite, and that good is not something to let go of despite the scars and wounds he's accumulated throughout his life. Her love, tender and meticulous, has strengthened him in ways that, even with his crooked leg, he will be able to better face the challenges of his life—and help teach others to do the same.

And challenges will come; the world doesn't wait for change, after all, and I think that's the hardest thing for me to put down in this novella. Ben is healing from the past, and looking forward to the future, but the present is full of changes that might seem good or bad, but either way, they can still bring us the best blessings.

When you are caught behind in your struggles, it can be hard to move along with time, and that's why unchanging things of truth, beauty, and goodness are so critical to use as mile markers, as well as progress. The world is changing, yet we still must find the good, the beautiful, and the true, and cling to it even as our ability to do just that wanes and waxes.

I truly hope you have enjoyed this series, and I love to think that leaving you here will give you plenty of ideas for your own stories of Ben and Marguerite going on missions with Tho and Thuy, and perhaps Ella, Ferdy, and all the others, too.

I hope you will look forward to my next series. It is always a miracle to me, to find familiar eyes on my work.

Until We Meet Again,

C. S. Johnson

SAMPLE READING

Chapter 1 *from*

DRAGON TEARS

A COMPANION NOVELLA TO

THE ALLIANCE OF THE DRAGON SWORD

※   ※   ※   ※

C. S. Johnson

THE ORDER OF THE CRYSTAL DAGGERS

CHAPTER ONE

※ ※ ※ ※

No one ever paid attention to a Ghost.

By the time I was twelve, I was used to how often eyes slid over me and the others as we went about our work. We were considered an essential, if regrettable, part of life in Laena, but as odd as that may sound, that was just how things were. In many ways, it was an understandable situation, too.

The Ghost Children of the Laenite Tribe were children who were born out of wedlock, orphaned at a young age, or even on the rare occasion, abandoned by our parents. The "Ghost" moniker was rumored to have been a jest originally, but as we were the remnants of incomplete lives, forgotten dreams, or abandoned mistakes, it was a label that carried a cruel truth.

In our community, where faith came first and family came second, Ghost Children were largely an afterthought.

However, the others and I did not allow this to be a point of contention between us and other Laenites. It wasn't as though the world and its realities left us unprepared. The Creator had given us a beautiful place to live and thrive, but because of sin, darkness, and despair, imperfections and abuses, there was an endless, growing chasm between humanity and divinity—all of this was unable to be ignored or denied. Our religion taught us to embrace our positions as the invisible shadows of our society, and through our work, even if it was not acknowledged, we kept the light burning ever more brightly.

To us, this was only right, since we were the adopted children of Ceru, the Great Sea Serpent and the Water Dragon Guardian of Laena.

Like the other Ghosts, Ceru took me in as an abandoned baby and gave me a bed, clothes, food, and a traditional education. It was thanks to Ceru that I had grown up surrounded by the hills of my home, where snowy mountains bled into waterfalls like open wounds and flowers dotted the ravines all throughout spring.

The arrangement had a sacred name in the ancient tongue, but the Laenites often referred to it as a Life Debt. Ceru saved my life when he adopted me, so it was my duty to serve and honor him.

Since I was a baby when my parents left me, I would be released from my Life Debt in my seventeenth year; if he'd saved my life as a grown adult, I would have been honor-bound to serve him for seven years or until he released me from my debt.

On my fourteenth Adoption Day—a Ghost Child's equivalent of a birthday—I received my main job assignment with the medic healers of Cathedral City. One year had passed since then, and ever since I started, I had enjoyed learning all I could about tending to different wounds and injuries, caring dutifully to the last moments of a dying life, and educating my patients on their recovery needs and expectations. Much like how I'd been drawn to Ceru's underground nest, I felt drawn toward my work as a healer.

Even when we lost a community member to disease or old age, I was greatly comforted by Ceru's assurance that such souls had entered into a better place; it was said the Dragon of Death would carry faithful souls to the Eternal Hall of the Creator, where we would live in endless joy. In this way, our grief was not without hope, and even in our sadness, I still found a gleam of goodness.

By far my favorite part of the job was helping the new mothers. I envied them the most, despite their obvious discomfort and their childbearing pain. The babies I helped birth made my heart flutter and ache at the same time, and while I had no husband to marry or admirer to court, I imagined falling in love wasn't so different from how I felt seeing that first glimpse of new, created life.

Each time I handed a mother her new baby, I felt a spark of fulfillment as much as a twang of longing.

I was grateful for what I had been given, I truly was; but as much as I loved Ceru and my home, my job, and my friends, I desperately wanted a family of my own.

There was something so alluring about the thought of running my own household, having a husband coming home to my hugs and kisses, and adding children to the world who were born out of the mutual adoration in my marriage.

It was so easy to picture that perfection inside my mind, even if I didn't have any idea what my future husband would look like.

Still, that only added to some of the mysterious allure. One day my husband could be tall and tan, with a large frame and soft eyes; the next he could have long hair and dimples that hugged his smiles. I didn't mind if he was long and lanky, or if he was short and stocky; as long as he loved me, I would love him more than anything else in the world, and we would never be happy unless we were together.

"Thessa! What are you doing?"

At the sound of Mother Nia's voice, I blinked, and my daydreams blurred into the scene before me, where I was tending to a sleeping patient. I was using a damp cloth to cool down a man's feverish brow, but I'd been caught up in thinking of tending to my own children in such a loving manner that I'd failed to notice the water was being so thickly applied, it was soaking his pillow.

"Oh." I quickly stepped away and gave Mother Nia a sheepish look.

THE ORDER OF THE CRYSTAL DAGGERS

"You're going to drown him if you're not careful." Her mouth was firmly set, but her ancient eyes lit up with a hidden laugh as she moved to adjust her habit.

"Well, it wouldn't be the worst thing to happen to him today," I replied with a joking smile.

Mother Nia clicked her tongue. "Impertinent girl," she murmured, but I saw her struggle to compose herself; I counted my retort as a win when she turned away from me.

From across the room, another voice spoke up in scolding tones. "If you ask me, Thessa's too distracted to work tonight."

I glared over at Kana, not surprised to see the disapproval on her otherwise perfect face. Kana was another Ghost who worked with me in the healer station. She was a little younger than me by a few months, but despite our similarities, I knew we would never be friends. We got along out of ritualistic necessity, even when I could see the underlying hints of her animosity.

Times like this.

"Forgive me, Mother Nia," I replied dutifully, lowering my eyes until I was absolved for my inattention.

No one ever paid attention to a Ghost—not unless we were doing something wrong. In my case, it did not help that Kana was quick to point out my shortcomings.

"Yes, yes, child." Mother Nia's normal reserved expression had returned by the time she waved away my meaningless apology. "Now, hurry. The pillow needs to be changed out quickly. We don't want Zebedee to get a cold."

"I will." I shot Kana a determined look.

"Perhaps I should take over for her tonight," Kana offered. "It is Thessa's Adoption Day, after all."

THE ORDER OF THE CRYSTAL DAGGERS

"That's true," I said, keeping my tone agreeable but not affirming. "But I can still work. My meeting with Father Ephyras isn't for another hour at least."

Kana held steady. "But if you're endangering the patients—"

"I'm sure Thessa won't let it happen again," Mother Nia said with a small, labored sigh. "And she's hardly endangering Zebedee, Kana. Honestly, if a man his age can survive falling into a ravine during combat drills, I'm sure a little extra water won't bother him. Now, be silent, girls, and get back to the tasks you've been assigned."

Mother Nia's face wrinkled as she gave us a warning glance and then shuffled out of the room.

Kana sneered at me before she went back to changing the bedsheets of another empty cot.

I felt heavy-hearted as Kana ignored me. I wasn't sure why we always seemed to have such trouble between us.

Kana was well-known for her good looks and intelligence. She had a larger group of friends than I did, and despite the rule of forbidden favorites, many of the priests and nuns around Cathedral City gushed over her more often than not.

Pia once told me that Kana hated being younger than me, and while I thought that was just silly, it was technically the one thing she would never accomplish over me—she could easily do a better job with our studies and accomplish more in the medical station. When it came to looking the part, Kana was organized, put-together, and always on time. I was always running a little late, my robes were a little wrinkled from sleeping in Ceru's mountain nest, and cleaning my room was a chore and a half.

"Did I hear that girl right? It's your Adoption Day?"

Zebedee stirred in his bed, and as I turned to face him, I saw him looking up at me with wonder.

THE ORDER OF THE CRYSTAL DAGGERS

"Yes, sir." I was glad he was awake; I wouldn't have to work as hard to get the pillow out from underneath him. "I'll be headed to the Cathedral after I'm done here."

"You should go then." Zebedee gave me a half-smile, one that looked painful from underneath the thick bandage on his head. "It's your fifteenth year, isn't it? Some young man will surely be ecstatic to have you as his bride."

Since we had been friendly for months, I gave Zebedee a quick kiss on the cheek. "I'm sure I can make an old man happy that I'm his medic."

Kana let out a discreet cough, and without looking, I knew she was rolling her eyes at me as Zebedee laughed.

"I'm surprised you're feeling so well. Especially since you had a rough tumble," I said. "Your first commander was horrified by the sight of you falling off the rocks."

"Ah, well … I should've been expecting it," Zebedee said. "Ceru's getting old, too, Thessa. His city and Laena itself are starting to crumble."

I felt a lump in my throat. The High Priests taught us through their records of history and prophecies that one day, the Age of Dragons would be over, and a new order would begin through bloodshed and sacrifice.

There was not much I doubted Ceru could handle—but the word of the Creator was not to be ignored, either.

But surely, I told myself, there were times when it was best to ignore such theories? Ceru, while he was old, had me and the other Ghosts by his side. We loved him, and I knew we would continue taking care of him for many years to come.

On the other hand, Zebedee was an old man, and perhaps he was just trying to massage his own ego by saying the main island of Laena was starting to weaken.

"Now, now," I said calmly, "Saying such things won't push Ceru to love you any more than he already does. I'm sure you'll get a dragon tear if he hears you need it."

"I doubt I'll need it. Ceru likely needs them more than I do, the way things are looking," Zebedee said, grimacing with pain. "But I'll take some painkillers if you have them ready."

I did my best to brush off his concern for Ceru. Zebedee was an older man, and stubborn, too. I wouldn't be able to convince him Ceru was fine, no matter how long I spent arguing with him.

But if nothing else, Zebedee was right. Painkillers would help. "I'll go and retrieve them for you."

Zebedee nodded. "After that, promise me you'll go and see Father Ephyras. I know you're eager to have your marriage arranged, but the community wants to hear who the very lucky man will be just as much as you do."

"All right." My cheeks flushed over with humbled pleasure, even if I doubted he was correct on that point, too. "Thank you, Zebedee."

True to my word, I finished my last chore for the night and headed out. Even Mother Nia seemed glad Zebedee had gotten me to agree to leave early. Both of them offered their blessings as I left, and the memory of their quiet, sincere affection kept me warm as I moved through the streets of Cathedral City.

A few others waved at me, and I waved back, surprised by the attention.

Maybe Zebedee wasn't entirely incorrect.

I was still a Ghost, but now that I was fifteen, and it was my Adoption Day, I was starting to become more of a real person in the eyes of the community.

THE ORDER OF THE CRYSTAL DAGGERS

The sun was still high enough in the sky I could see clearly all the way to the top of the Hallowed Mountain. As I walked down from the medic station, I sighed contentedly at the sights before me.

The market in the city was bustling with a lively energy, like the invisible echoes of a song, and its rhythm was one with the beat of my own heart.

The Cathedral of the Great Sea Serpent was a massive building, built at the bottom of the Hallowed Mountain, where Ceru resided and labyrinthian springs of water kept him connected to the rest of the world. On either side of the mountain, a crescent arm of land curled around, making a natural harbor, where community members would keep their fishing ships and other seacraft. Behind the mountain, there was the forest of Laena, with its various trails, and then even further back, there was mostly farmland where the people of Laena peacefully resided. There were some other mountains, too, and then at the back of the island, there was the Great Waterfall of Laena. It was at the opposite end of the island from the Cathedral, running down the middle of the island's natural plateau.

At the bottom of the waterfall was marked the border between us and the home of Fuergo, the Fire Dragon Republic of Kator. They filled in a large chunk of the rest of the main continent, though there were several ongoing border disputes and historical claims with the Earth Dragon, Yla, and her nation, Atlaris, or so I'd heard.

The leaders of the Laenite Tribe had long ago decided not to interfere with the affairs of the world, and it was precisely because of Yla and Fuergo's various forms of warfare that history could attest to the wisdom of that decision.

"Thessa, there you are! Good heavens, did you hear?"

I barely had time to prepare myself before I found Philia rushing into me. She embraced me in a quick, sisterly hug,

THE ORDER OF THE CRYSTAL DAGGERS

which I tried to reciprocate before she began jumping up and down.

"What is it?" I asked, laughing at her wild enthusiasm before catching some myself. "Did you hear something about me for my Adoption Day?"

"Oh, that's right. That's today, too." Philia's pretty face ducked down in apologetic shame. "I forgot."

"There's no issue," I assured her, even though I felt a little disappointed. I hid my hurt from her and gripped her hands with some measure of excitement. "Tell me what's happening."

"Oh, Thessa, an Arian ship is pulling into the harbor." Philia grinned. "And it's a big one, too. Perhaps we will get to hear another concert, maybe? What do you think?"

"I don't know," I admitted, although I was intrigued.

The Arian Islands were our neighbors from across the Western Seas. They served under Aria, the Dragon of Air, and their kingdom was made on artificially connected islands. They were full of talented artists and musicians, known for their appreciation and desire for beauty throughout the rest of the world. Occasionally, they would visit other regions of the world to showcase their talents or expand their trade routes.

"Come and see," Philia said, tugging on my hands. "They should be at port in a few moments."

I hesitated only for a moment; I wanted to go to the Hallowed Mountain, back to where Father Siah and the High Priest would be waiting for me, along with a message from Ceru regarding my Adoption Day—a message which possibly would inform me of who I was to marry after my Life Debt was over.

THE ORDER OF THE CRYSTAL DAGGERS

But Philia kept pulling on me, and after I took a look at the water clock set up in front of the Cathedral, I saw I had a little time to indulge my friend.

"Come on, Thessa," Philia insisted. "Pia's already down there, and Davar and Edmun are headed that way, too. They were told to report there for their soldier training in full uniform, so you know it has to be something important."

"They were?" I began walking with Philia, watching as she bubbled over with pleasure. She was a little over a year younger than me, and I couldn't help but feel old as she tried to hold my hand and skip down the street.

"Oh, yeah," Philia said. "Pia's already down there because of her job, but she'll be let out by the time we get there. And I was let out of work early today since one of the younglings spit up on me."

"Ew." I shook her off my arm. "You should've told me that earlier."

"I was wearing an apron." Philia nearly doubled over in laughter as I let out a silent prayer of thanks that I'd been appointed to work with the healers.

My friends and fellow Ghosts were old enough that each had been assigned a job, but I loved mine the most. Philia worked with the younger children as an assistant teacher; she would be promoted to a primary teacher in a few more years, and then she would work until she was married. Pia, her twin sister, worked down by Cathedral City's main port, overseeing fisherman and food production. I still saw them frequently, despite my longer shifts, but it was harder to keep up with my friends Davar and Edmun, since in addition to their jobs, boys were called to train as part of the Laenite Tribe's armed forces, but when we had a chance to meet, we did. As much as it interrupted my Adoption Day, I smiled at the thought of seeing them again.

"Ooh, Thessa, remember last time the Arians came? They brought us spools of fine cloth and those lovely shoes," Philia gushed. "And that jewelry, too!"

"You know Ghosts like us aren't supposed to draw attention to ourselves," I reminded her. "Why get so excited?"

"I'm more excited for you," Philia said. "Your Adoption Day is today. Surely, you'll get your marriage arranged, and as a bride, you can be as extravagant as you'd like."

As we made our way down to the port, Philia continued to babble, filling my head with even more daydreams and ideas. I couldn't help but allow her ideas to whisk my imagination away into another world, and even the sight of the Arian ship tying off into port couldn't fully bring me back to attention.

"Philia, Thessa, over here!"

Over the gathering crowds, I heard Davar calling out to us from the adjacent dock. I could see the dark burgundy of his hair sticking out from his helm. Philia had been right, it seemed; Davar was in his full armor, decked out in his gilded breastplate and the formal, silver-embroidered leather underneath his chainmail.

We made our way over to the adjacent dock as the Arian ship crept closer to shore.

"Where's Edmun?" I asked as we approached.

"He went to go with some of the other Ghosts," Davar said. "Father Piet ordered him to get Cathedral City's best guesthouses ready."

"So you know who's coming? What have you heard?" Philia asked Davar as we greeted each other.

"You wouldn't believe me if I told you." Davar straightened with pride, clearly enjoying having the upper hand over us; it was a rare occasion. "I've heard some of the port keepers talking about it."

"Well, tell us, then," Philia insisted. "Don't be cruel and make us wait. Is it another concert tour?"

"No, and praise the Creator for that." Davar stuck out his tongue in light disgust. He had no patience for music, although I had to wonder if that was intentional. Thanks to Philia, who often took to gossiping, we knew that Davar's father had likely been an Arian singer.

"Word has it that the Arian king has sent his highest-ranking ambassador here, and the ship's marking proves it," Davar said. He pointed toward the mast, where a royal purple flag waved in the breeze. "See the silver design on it? That's the coat of arms for the Rico family."

"It's so elegant," Philia said with a happy sigh. "I wonder what they've brought us? Maybe a new flag for Cathedral City's public square? That would be lovely. Father Dion was just mentioning about seeing to the City's upgrades."

"I don't know," I said, suddenly noticing the small legion of troops standing on the top deck. "They've come with soldiers."

"Well, I doubt it's an invasion if you're worried about that. They wouldn't be that foolish," Philia said. "Laena is very self-sufficient, and that's largely because our troops help protect us."

Davar grinned. "Of course we do, so you're welcome."

"Who says I was talking about you?" Philia teased. "You're still at a minor rank."

"Still better than you," Davar snapped back.

"Well, it's not my fault that women don't fight, is it?"

"Women like you are the reason we fight. We protect the rest of the world from having to deal with the likes of you."

I bit back a sigh as I ignored them. Philia and Davar had always been close, and with each passing year, I often wondered if they fought to prove they weren't secretly in love. Due to the mysterious nature of their heritage, Ghost Children were not often allowed to marry each other. Ceru would be the one who would have the final say in that matter, but given the odds, I couldn't blame Philia and Davar for their squabbles. Smaller pains in the present helped to possibly avoid larger ones in the future.

That was part of the reason the Laenites did not encourage some of the courting rituals many of the other countries and nations had, too. From what I knew of other nations' temporal relationships, divorces, and dating disasters, I was honestly relieved. I wanted a lasting love, a love that I could rely on to strengthen and support me; something I could add to and something that could give back something even more beautiful.

As Davar and Philia continued to tease and taunt each other, I kept my eyes on the approaching ship. It was a grand one, with silk-lined sails and intricate carvings along both sides. The Arians were known for their spectacle as much as their presentation.

I squinted as I saw a soldier moving across the ship, headed for the point of the bow.

The sun's setting light flickered over his helmed brow like a kiss of lightning. I watched, intrigued, as he took out a small flute and began to play.

The trill of the music fluttered down from on high in a lovely wave, making my heart lurch inside my chest.

I had always adored music. Both in my darkest midnights and my bright moments of joy, I would sing songs and find strength and sustenance.

I looked for the source of the song, and found myself staring at a man near the maidenhead of the ship.

The flute player held himself upright with confidence and flare, and as I watched him play, I almost wished I'd learned how to play an instrument, too. I was part of the worship choir as a singer, but I had no great talent.

I decided right then and there that if I ever had the time, I would write Ceru a song I could sing while another played the flute.

"Oh, that's beautiful." Philia leaned against my shoulder as she finally took notice of the music.

"Please, he's not that good," Davar argued, which sparked another argument with Philia.

I heard another shout from behind the flute player, and the music halted in mid-song.

A breath of stillness and silence took over.

And then, in the blink of an eye, the Arian boat suddenly slammed against the receiving dock.

The dock's wooden titles snapped. Ropes alternatively tightened and lagged, while several others called out everything from orders to screams of horror.

My eyes widened in shock as I watched the flute player. He wobbled dangerously atop the maidenhead of the ship, and just like before, a long, seemingly endless moment passed as we watched, transfixed by the danger.

And then fate finally gave its verdict.

Philia gasped, and even Davar's mouth dropped open as the flute player lost his battle with his balance, and he fell forward off the ship.

I closed my eyes as he met the water's surface in a devastating *splash*.

THE ORDER OF THE CRYSTAL DAGGERS

Thank you for reading! Please leave a review for this book and check out www.csjohnson.me for other books and updates!

THE ORDER OF THE CRYSTAL DAGGERS